FALLING FOR THE SINGE MOM

THE GREAT LOVELY FALLS - BOOK ONE

ALIE GARNETT

12-153-44 PUBLISHING

Edited by Thoth Editing

Images © DepositPhotos – cybernesco & iStock - dragana991

Cover Design © Designed with Grace

For R

MEET THE LOVELY'S

Seraphina Lovely – 35-year-old who is divorced and the Director of HR, mom of two, step-mom to five, secretly in love with an unnamed co-worker who spends his days looking for new ways to annoy her.

Harper Lovely - 30-year-old who is a Personal assistant to a jerk, CEO/CFO/just plain C of Lovely Catering with Lucy and boss of all her sisters.

Mabel Lovely - 28-year-old who is a Professor of Children's Lit and homebody. Older of the twins.

Lucy Lovely - 28-year-old who works for her sister at Lovely Catering, cleans offices, and wild child of the family. Younger of the twins.

Agatha Lovely - 26-year-old who is an amazing artist and mediocre bartender looking for a job.

Buzz Lovely – 25-year-old Reporter for the times, youngest and most outgoing of the big girls.

Emmaline Lovely – 15-year-old sullen teen, Sera's first born.

Violet Lovely – 8-year-old upbeat, outgoing artist. Sera's baby who isn't a baby anymore.

CHAPTER ONE

"IT WOULDN'T BOTHER you so much if you weren't such an uptight prude!" Harrison Dean yelled at the HR director from across her desk. Sure, it was unprofessional, but they had known each other for ten years now, and she was what she was. He was just man enough to say it out loud.

The desk between them held a computer, an open blue file, and nothing else—just a smooth, gray oak surface devoid of any personality, just like its owner. There wasn't even a picture of her family or friends. No items from home to remind her not to take work so seriously. Nothing.

This woman needed something that would take her mind off work once in a while. More than once in a while.

"Oh, please, Harrison. You were having sex in the *conference room*. That's not acceptable behavior anywhere. Should I have to point out that you're one of the top lawyers in the company? If this gets out, everyone will be doing it! And if it gets out, I'll have to have this conversation with everyone, and I don't want to talk about this more than once."

Seraphina Lovely gave as good as she got. A certifiable prude, but not a wallflower.

This wasn't their first fight, nor would it be their last. He and the blonde had even had an argument like this before. In fact, this wasn't even the worst one they'd been in over the years. They had the ability to rub each other the wrong way over almost every issue. It could be because he liked to rile her up just for fun. Pushing her buttons was a past-time now, and he was good at it.

"Because if I do it, everyone will?" Harrison stated with annoyance.

He couldn't not use her given name, even though he knew she hated it. She always corrected people, saying that it was "Sera with an E." Sometimes she even added that she would not respond to Seraphina, but she always did. The fact that it said "Sera" on her door was a bit of annoyance to him. He loved that her name didn't match her personality at all.

In his mind, a Seraphina was an overly friendly woman who had little to no opinion of her own—a trophy wife. But this Seraphina was the complete opposite of that, even if her body was built to be a trophy wife, with curves in all the right places. Her bland color palette of mostly black and gray couldn't cover that up.

"Yes, Harrison. You're a role model around here. Lord knows why, but the younger lawyers look up to you. I, for one, think you're overrated."

She looked up at him with her bright blue eyes and a small smile on her face, a perma-smile he liked to call it. It was always there; even now, when she was pissed off, she was still smiling.

"I'm worth looking up to," he stated with a smarmy smirk and watched her shake her head, which caused her long blonde hair to slip around her shoulders.

"You're a horny asshole who'll nail anything that isn't nailed down." Her breasts heaved with her anger under her steel-gray blouse. It also made her cheeks a rosy red. Maybe that was why he liked to fight with her so much—who wouldn't love this reaction?

"At least I remember the last time I had sex. You don't even remember how to spell it, much less how to do it!"

He knew nothing about her sex life, but she had been married for as long as he had known her. Longer, in fact. He only remembered her being pregnant once years ago, but he might have missed a few. He didn't keep up with Mrs. Lovely's life. He was sure there was nothing interesting about it at all.

"What does my sex life have to do with yours?" She crossed her arms in defense, drawing his eyes to her breasts. They were a special kind of nice, for a sexless prude. Her husband was a lucky guy on that front.

"Absolutely nothing, thank god!" His eyes went back to the safety of her face before she noticed. Would she like that? Him getting caught looking at the HR director's tits?

"Oh, please. Kylie Nash is twenty years old. Is that your yardstick for what you want in a woman? A kid barely out of high school? You are thirty-six years old. You could have a kid her age!" Her words finally brought her to her feet. Everyone knew that when she stood up, shit was going down. Nobody got fired while she was sitting.

Now they were closer to the same height. She was tall for a woman, mostly legs, though with the desk between them, he couldn't see them below her usual knee-length black skirt. But he had seen them many, many times before and didn't need to see them to know what they looked like. Good, they looked good.

Leaning towards her, he stated, "You're just jealous that you have to hurry home to the same dick every night—no variety. Are you missing that in your life? Did you ever even have variety in your life?"

Harrison had no idea how old she was. Maybe his age, maybe not. Knowing her for so long had made her a fixture in his life, nothing more. He didn't think about her at all other than as the HR director … a pain in the ass one.

"I will not discuss my personal life with you."

"Let's not discuss my personal life either then," he countered.

"You keep it out of my offices, and I will. Do whatever the hell you want on your time. Not here." She pointed a long, elegant finger at the desk between them.

"Has she filed a complaint?" He had a right to know if she had. He knew the rules and laws surrounding sexual harassment.

"No," she admitted, her eyes going to her black computer screen.

She probably wished it hadn't gone black during their fight in case she got an email about it. She would've loved that.

"Then, she was willing." He smirked. She had nothing on him.

"I don't give a rat's ass if she was willing or not. It was in the damn conference room. Keep your pants on at work. Hell, keep all your clothes on!" She sat down in her chair and crossed her legs before sliding her chair into position under the desk.

"I can't help it if the ladies love me." He turned to leave her since he had won. If no report was filed, he had no issues.

"Just not in the office." She barked after him as if he was listening to her.

"Tell your dick hi when you see him tonight." Harrison smirked again as he walked out of her office without another goodbye. He knew the discussion wasn't over, and neither was the fight—just put off for another time.

On his way back to his office on the opposite end of the floor, he wondered how she had even found out about him and Kylie. Who had seen it or heard it? Whoever it was, was lying. He and Kylie had not had sex in the conference room, nor anywhere else. Maybe some very heavy petting, but so far, he hadn't done anything with her. She was twenty years old, for god's sake.

At closer to forty than thirty, he wasn't looking for a relationship with someone not even old enough to drink in a bar. Not that what she lacked in age, she didn't make up for with eagerness over the last few months, but he was so far a hard no on that. Sex wasn't an issue; he could find a woman for that easily. No need to even look at work.

All he wanted from the woman was to be a semi-decent personal assistant. She was failing on that end and failing miserably.

There was no way he was telling Seraphina Lovely that. He was happy for her to think he was getting laid right under her nose. It probably gave her something to be hot and bothered about. Lord, she probably needed it.

Walking into his office, he hurried past Kylie Nash, who was sitting at her desk but not working. In fact, she had done very little work since she had started there. As far as he knew, she had other plans for her time at the office. They ended with a career that didn't involve work, and he was not signing up for that.

"What happened?" she demanded breathily; her breasts thrust his way as she said it. Not that the pale pink dress did anything to hide those breasts or anything else, for that matter. It was painted on her.

"I took care of it, but whatever happened in that room is over. In fact, it was over before it even started. I'm not interested," he repeated what he had told her earlier in the day when she had nearly stripped him out of his pants before he could stop her.

It had been a difficult conversation then, and it was just as bad now. It seemed that whatever school she went to didn't cover inappropriate office behavior.

"I wonder who told?" she asked coyly, and Harrison suddenly knew exactly who had told everyone they'd had sex. He was looking at her, but not her breasts, because he wasn't interested in those. They had nothing on Seraphina Lovely's, who had won that contest without even entering the competition.

"Kylie, you know I'm not interested in you, correct?" he asked the blonde, whose hair was also nothing like Sera's. This one had no wave, no body ... nothing he could sink his fingers into.

"Harrison, I don't think you mean that. We're good together," said the twenty-year-old who knew nothing about him except that he had money and a career that made him more money—unless she ruined his career before he could make any more.

"No, we are not. I'm already dating someone." Harrison half-lied. For a while, he had been sleeping with someone, but that wasn't going anywhere.

Since his divorce four years before, he hadn't really "dated" anyone. Yes, he had screwed around a lot, but there hadn't been a hint of a relationship. After over a decade of marriage, he was swinging single and happy about it. He wasn't going to start something with a woman who a worked for him. Barely a woman at that.

"You've never said anything about her." Kylie actually pouted.

"Because I don't like to talk about my personal life at work. I like to keep it professional here." He used Seraphina's lines on her. Lord knows he'd heard it a time or two.

"She doesn't have to know," she purred, her ability to change course surprising him.

She was like a bad cold: hard to shake until you infected everyone. "I would know, and I am not that kind of man."

Okay, that was an outright lie. His marriage had ended because he had cheated, and more than once. But this chick needn't know that. Maybe she already knew; a lot of people in the office did. He hadn't kept the end of his marriage a secret. When it was happening, he was more than willing to say anything about it, anything at all.

Kylie frowned. "I don't know what to say."

"Well, I have to get to work if you don't mind." He pointed to his office. Before she could respond, he went in and shut the door. He hoped that after today, this wouldn't be an issue again.

Except it was an on-going issue that didn't seem to be going away, no matter how many times he told her no.

CHAPTER TWO

THE GROG WAS PACKED when Sera Lovely walked in at 6 p.m. It was a dingy corner bar with a karaoke machine, sticky tables, and watered-down drinks. The service was slow, and the beers on tap were always questionable. Looking around, she tried to come up with why it was crowded. It was the Grog—why would anyone willingly be there?

She lived three blocks away, so this was her bar. If she wanted a drink in the evening, she came here. People at the bar should greet her by name and ask about her day. It wasn't great, but it was her bar.

She hadn't even bothered to change before coming in today; she needed alcohol, and she needed it badly. If there was a drink called "sex on the desk," she would be getting a double. Instead, she tried to remember what she had last time. It was good and strong, and exactly what she needed. But sadly, she had no idea what it was called, or even what was in it. But that was definitely what she wanted right now.

At the surprising full bar, she leaned over one of the empty stools to knock hard on the scarred wood three times as if it were a front door. Instantly, the bartender turned to her and headed her way. His easy smile made her day a little brighter, or maybe it was because he controlled the booze, and they were closer than ever.

"Hey, Sera. Your usual?" Okay, maybe she knew some of the bartenders. Cliff had spent some time in her house over the last few months. Not with her, but with her daughter, Lucy. Sometimes it was like he was the son she never had and never wanted, but was there anyway. Like a leech.

"Yes, Cliff." She smiled at him in appreciation. Now she didn't have to remember anything. He was a good-looking guy but not her type. Mostly because he was also the most annoying man she had ever met. He'd never met a woman he didn't hit on, including her. His only save gracing was that he was genuine with his words.

"Bad day? You didn't even change." He set the glass near her.

"Yeah, it was a shitshow. What's going on tonight?" She waved at the people. It was busier than on a Friday night when they had a live band. For a Thursday, it was unacceptable.

"We made some sort of twenty-five best bars in the city list. An error, I'm sure, but every shitty douchebag has been in here for the last few days. Tips are good." Cliff said, not caring that someone might hear him. That's how Cliff was.

"Are my girls making good tips?" she asked him, taking a sip of her drink. It was the one she had been thinking of, and Cliff had made it perfectly.

"Luce works at eight, and Buzz is floating around. Agatha is in at midnight, and Harper worked this afternoon." He named off almost all her adult girls. The only one missing was currently a university professor who didn't wait tables anymore. She had a "real job," as she liked to say. Except nearly all her girls had a "real" job. Bartending and waitressing were for money, fun, and free booze, which gave their mother free booze also—an added bonus.

"Thanks, Cliff. I want another, and point me to a table with some Lovely ladies at it." Cliff saluted her with a cocky grin. He was nuts.

When a second drink was in her hand, Cliff pointed her to the corner, of course. Buzz and Lucy were leaning against the wall, each in a booth with their legs stretched out in front of them. It didn't matter how full the bar was; they had a table, and they were not sharing.

Lucy saw her first and waved, swinging her feet down from the bench. Sliding in beside her, Sera set her glasses down carefully, not wanting to spill her drinks.

"Bad day, Mom?" Buzz asked from across the table, nodding at her double drinks.

"Shitshow," Sera repeated what she had told Cliff. "Cliff made them extra strong for me."

Buzz, whose real name was Beatrix, just laughed and took a drink from one, then made a face and shook her head. Buzz hated girly drinks, but they were Sera's favorite.

Buzz was as flighty and interesting as her name. The redhead was short and constantly trying new things. She had just spent the day waitressing but was actually a reporter for the Times. She didn't get any good stories, but it was only a matter of time before she made her name. For now, she was busy all the time, just the same.

With her hair up in a ponytail, she looked younger than her twenty-five years and usually got carded when they went out. Not here, though. Maybe that was because her older sisters worked here and always gave their little sisters a slide when the need was there.

Buzz was the youngest of the stepdaughters, but her personality was closest aligned to Sera's. That wasn't saying much since four of the five were outgoing and chatty like Sera. But maybe she was reading too much into her parenting skills. They were half grown before she even met them, so maybe it wasn't all her.

Beside her, Lucy's fingers bounced on the table like she was missing her piano. Lucy was always in motion; her body never stopped moving, except to sleep. Currently, Lucy was a caterer with her sister Harper, but she also cleaned office buildings in her off time.

The two sisters at the table looked nothing alike. Even their brown eyes were not even close to the same shade. Lucy's dark brown hair was up in the same style as her sister's, and the yellow T-shirt she wore was as bold and bright as she was.

All Sera's stepdaughters looked different but were supposed to be the product of the same union—something Sera had questioned since meeting them fifteen years before. Not that she would ever get an answer since their father had abandoned them to her within weeks of their marriage, and their birth mother was already long gone by then.

"So, what evil thing happened to make the HR director need two drinks?" Lucy also tried the beverage. She shrugged at the taste and went back to hers: a beer in a formerly frosty mug, by the looks of it.

"Sex in the conference room." She took a long-awaited drink.

"You?" Buzz asked with a questioning eyebrow raised.

Sera tried not to spit out the liquid but found herself choking on it as she swallowed it. It burned when it went down, making her suck in breaths of air. Sometimes drinking was a hazard when her kids were around. Eating could turn out the same way.

"Fuck, Buzz. No!" she finally said through the burn. Both girls were laughing at her because they knew what had happened.

"Two drinks, Sera?" Harper knocked her sister's feet to the floor as she slid into the booth with them.

The oldest of the five was the one that closest resembled Sera: blonde hair and brown eyes, still different than any of her sisters. Harper could have been Sera's own daughter, except for the five years in age that actually separated them. In reality, Buzz was only ten years younger than Sera, so having any of them as a real daughter was impossible, but she had gotten them through marriage, so they were all hers anyway. They might be stepdaughters, but the step was very small, just how Sera liked it.

"What's so funny?" Harper pulled Sera's second drink towards her and took a sip.

"Sera having sex in the conference room," Lucy stated, straight-faced.

"Doesn't sound comfortable, but to each his own." Harper looked at the drink and shook her head at the taste but took another sip anyway.

Buzz did a stage whisper as she leaned into her older sister. "She says it wasn't her."

"Too bad. She hasn't been getting lucky lately. We all know how crabby she gets when she isn't getting laid." Harper pointed at her with her glass, not noticing the evil look her mom was sending her.

"I will have you all know I got laid just last weekend," she said loudly enough that the table heard, and maybe the next table over.

"Tell me you did not sleep with that douchebag." Harper shook her head at her.

"I did not." Sera laughed as she tried to grab her extra drink back . "I ditched him and met this guy at the bar." Okay, so she lied. It had been a while, but if the girls knew that, they would set her up tonight, and she didn't want that.

Yes, at work, she pretended to be married and had been when she had first started her job. In fact, she had been married until she was almost thirty, but her actual marriage had lasted around a month. That was when Bradford Lovely had gone from teaching English at the university across town to teaching at one in Peru.

The sudden transfer had surprised everyone, including his new bride and his five preteen-to-teenage girls. At nineteen, she watched the backside of her spouse as he headed to his assignment that was supposed to have only lasted a few months, and she hadn't seen him since. Once a year, she got a phone call from him to check on his girls. That was fifteen years ago. Six years ago, when Buzz had graduated from high school, she had finally divorced him. He hadn't contested it, and she hadn't used a lawyer from the firm she worked at.

So, she was now happily divorced and had custody of her five step-daughters, who were all adults now. But at this point, they all lived at home with her, so she got to see them every day.

"Proof!" Buzz demanded from the corner.

"I have none. It was a one-night stand," Sera replied. *What proof was there?*

"You should find someone tonight! I mean, that was last weekend. A long time ago," Lucy said in all seriousness. "I'll keep my eye out for someone. I think you want someone fun and adventurous."

"And how do you pick out the adventurous ones?" Sera asked her. Lucy did usually find adventurous ones from what she had noticed over the years, so maybe there was a trick to it.

Sera know that at least two of her children had been sexually active when she met them, and at the time, they were all under fifteen. But with an absent-minded father and an actually absent mother, the five girls had no supervision at all. No way was a nineteen-year-old getting them under control, so she did her best, and now they were all sexually active. But it didn't interfere with school or jobs, and condoms were handed out like candy since they were young.

"You look into their eyes and wink. If they wink back, you've found one. That's the signal. I can't believe you haven't heard that before." Lucy stated, all serious.

"I call bullshit, Lucy Maud." Sera called her out on her joke.

"Actually, I've heard that also," Harper said with a straight face, still drinking Sera's second drink.

"Et tu, Harper?" she snapped at her oldest stepdaughter.

It was times like these that she loved being their mom. She loved being in the middle of this mess of women. They made her shitty day go away within minutes with laughs and smiles.

CHAPTER THREE

"I BET you I can get every woman in that back booth to take their shirts off in ten minutes." The man behind the bar said with a grin. Harrison looked up and watched the dark-haired man as he put a whiskey neat in front of him. "Hundred bucks."

Harrison turned to the table of laughing women. Not one seemed drunk, and it was close to 6:30 p.m., so he doubted the man could do it. "Deal, but you can't go over there and talk to them."

The bartender looked him up and down and said, "Deal."

Harrison turned in his stool to watch the table in question. He wasn't missing this if it happened, and if not, he had a hundred dollars coming his way. The bar was packed as he had expected it to be —it had made a hottest bar list over the weekend. Not number one, but fifteen out of twenty-five wasn't all that bad. That was until you looked around. Then you wondered if it was one of the worst twenty-five in the city. It was nothing but a dive bar.

Harrison like a crowded bar every once in a while, but not all the time. His friend Jonas Raiden loved a trendy bar, and those were always crowded. Jonas was in town for the night and had wanted to get together, and here was where he had chosen, good or bad.

Jonas was late, and there were going to be some topless ladies in here soon. It wasn't late, but the women were really getting into the karaoke that was starting on the stage. Harrison hated trendy bars.

The blonde on the end was talking to a brunette, then snapped a quip to the blonde in front of her, and Harrison stopped breathing. Seraphina Lovely. It was her perma-smile giving the blonde a talking down. Harrison had been on the receiving end of enough of them to know what she was doing. He was surprised she would go off on her friends, if that's what they were.... She didn't seem the type to have friends.

Easy money, Harrison decided. No way was the prude of HR taking off her shirt. Maybe the other three. But not her, not here, not ever. She probably didn't even change clothes in her bedroom, needing to do it in the bathroom in case her husband saw her.

As a waitress carried over a tray of drinks and started to unload them, she talked to the group. They seemed to know her. When the waitress walked away, she grinned at Cliff at the bar and winked. Harrison's eyes snapped back to the table. The group was fighting and pointing at each other. Before he knew it, Seraphina Lovely was looking down and unbuttoning her steel-gray blouse. His eyes locked on seeing those breasts he had seen hints of for years.

He was so focused on her that when a blue shirt landed on top of her blonde head, he snapped his eyes to her tablemates to see two of the other three were already down to their bra's and waiting on the other two.

His eyes slid back to Seraphina's full breasts that were straining against the black lacy fabric. Her cleavage was deep enough to leave him wanting more. Before his very eyes, the bra was suddenly gone, covered by the blue T-shirt that had been on her head. Those glorious mounds were gone, and he missed them; wanted them back.

Where her black lace and breasts had been was now "Kantaty" in yellow. He didn't even know what that meant. The show was over, so he turned back to the bartender, who was also watching with a smirk on his face. Harrison wondered if the man was watching Seraphina Lovely also or one of the others.

"I lost. Red didn't remove hers." The bartender pulled a hundred from the cash register and handed it to him. His defeat didn't seem to bother him too much. Harrison's win wasn't all that satisfying either, now that the breasts were back in hiding.

"It's okay, man. Three of four is pretty good." Harrison slid the money back to him. He needed it more than Harrison did.

"Red's tits are pretty nice, but she likes to go braless, and it's too early in the night for her to forget." The bartender shrugged and took the money back.

Looking back at the table, Seraphina was now alone on her side. Right now, he wished she'd gone braless.

"Hey, man. What are you looking at? A chick?" Jonas slid onto the stool next to Harrison.

"No, just people watching," Harrison lied.

"This place looks great. Is it new?" Jonas took in the rest of the room, including the brunette from Seraphina's table singing her heart out to Shania Twain. The rest were watching her as well.

"I don't think so. Just caught fire." Harrison looked around and knew it was just a flash fire.

"It's cool, like an old dive bar. Exactly how one of those would look," Jonas replied.

Harrison knew it was an old dive bar; nothing special about it. Even the wait staff wasn't impressed with all the people, but he wasn't telling his buddy that. Let him believe what he wanted.

"I'm not feeling it." Harrison was having a hard time keeping his eyes off the back of the bar. Now it was only the blonde and the redhead sitting side by side—Seraphina was gone.

Looking around the room again, he hoped to see her, but she was gone. During the next hour, she didn't return to the table. Somehow, the vibe in the bar had changed, and he couldn't find anything good about it anymore. Not even when he noticed that her three friends were still there.

Had she gone home to her husband? Maybe he called and needed her home for him, or she just knew she had to get home before she stayed out too late. Harrison wondered if her husband was aware of her changing clothes at the bar. All he knew was that the man was probably going to see that black bra. For some reason, that just pissed Harrison off.

Since the bar no longer held the appeal it had before, he convinced Jonas that they should find bar fourteen on the list and see if it was any better. Jonas was up for the change, and they headed out, but not before he took one last look around the bar for a blonde in a blue T-shirt. Nothing.

CHAPTER FOUR

IT WAS CASUAL FRIDAY, which was always Sera's busiest day. Business casual and what you would wear to the bar to look for a fun night were not the same thing. But so many people had to be reminded of that every week—*every week!*

This was the reason she wore the same thing every day; no business casual for her. Not that she even thought about it after twelve years. Friday was just another day. Some weeks, it was the worst day of the week. Sera was happy with her gray skirt and lighter gray blouse; she liked to dress in black, white, and gray. At home, she wore everything but black. She didn't even have black jeans. It was color, color everywhere when she was home.

Her only issue with today's outfit was that she felt it smelt a little like bacon, as in Filet Mignon. Harper and Lucy had served it the week before at a private luncheon. One of her daughters had to have worn the skirt as she early-morning prepped before her second job. Last year, Sera had found her a personal assistant job that went from 4 a.m. until noon; perfect for a caterer … until said caterer borrowed her clothes and prepped in them, leaving her hungry and smelling all day.

At least they were happy with what they did. Her only goal as a mom was to have happy kids, and so far, she'd succeeded without using the pressure some parents put on kids.

Of course, Harrison's personal assistant, Kylie Nash, was on her list this week about her clothes, just like the week before. Walking into Harrison Dean's outer office, she was happy the couple wasn't having sex. Not that she thought that they had sex all the time, but what was the difference between a conference room and an office? It *was* casual Friday, and from what she'd heard about what Kylie was wearing, it was very casual Friday.

Pushing into the office, she saw the younger woman at her desk. Kylie's eyes were on her phone, and she wasn't even pretending to work. If Sera wasn't looking at close to fifty percent of her breasts, she would talk to the woman about what she did on company time. Instead, it was the breasts that steered the conversation.

"Kylie, we need to talk," she said to the younger woman … again.

"Mr. Dean and I have stopped our relationship." The younger woman looked up from her phone finally—she had no common sense at all.

"I hope so, Kylie. It's inappropriate, as is that dress." Sera looked at the red cocktail dress that left nothing to the imagination, and when she sat, everyone knew she wasn't wearing panties. Or at least the three people who called her about it had noticed. *At fucking work!*

"I'm sorry, Mrs. Lovely." Always with the "Mrs. Lovely" like she was a schoolteacher. But then again, the woman was twenty years old. Most likely, she had encountered teachers in the last two years. "I have a date tonight, and I don't have time to change before it."

A date surprised Sera since Kylie was supposed to be having a relationship with Harrison. Or maybe it was just a work thing, and they both had different partners in their personal life. Gross.

"That is not an acceptable excuse. When this happens, just change in the bathroom after you clock out. There's no need to wear that dress all day." She tried to explain what anyone should be able to figure out.

"Mr. Dean said it was okay this morning." She crossed her arms, and Sera was sure she was about to see some major boobage; one was sure to bounce free at any moment. It wouldn't be the first time, and it wouldn't be the last, but she always wished it was.

"Mr. Dean knows better, Kylie. Maybe you should just stick to business attire all the time. You're having a hard time with business casual," Sera reiterated.

Looking into Kylie's light blue doe eyes, Sera was planning for another night of drinks. After so many drinks, tomorrow would be an issue, but that was another day.

"What can I help you with today, Seraphina?" Harrison asked. He always called her by that name, to her annoyance.

It was the name parents gave to their children that they didn't want to grow any older than eleven. That was the age she stopped using it, and at thirty-six, she knew she should have changed it years before. Only Harrison called her it now, and he only did it because he knew she hated it. That was how he was.

"Just was telling Kylie here that her dress is inappropriate for work." She liked that Harrison at least never did casual Friday either. It seemed to be the one thing they both agreed on.

Mostly, he didn't like her, and she had no idea what she had done to deserve his bad side. She knew she'd been nothing but nice to him. Unless he truly needed to be talked to, she didn't. In fact, over the years, she had let him slide on some issues because he was a partner at the firm. Only when he really needed it did she bring it up to him.

"I told her you said it was okay." Kylie rushed to his side. For his part, he stepped away when she got too close.

"I didn't say it was exactly okay. I said it was okay this time," Harrison said to Kylie, not to Sera, talking to her like she was a child.

"I don't think it's okay this time, Harrison." Sera pointed out.

How could he not see that her outfit was completely unacceptable for the office? It was almost unacceptable for a date.

"You know what, Kylie? Seraphina is absolutely correct. You can take the rest of the day off, and don't wear that dress here again."

Sera's eyes swung to the man in amazement. Did he just do that? Just let her have over half a day off for misbehaving? It wasn't the first time she had done this, so she knew coming in that she was in the wrong.

"Thanks, Harrison." Kylie actually squealed and rushed over to Harrison and hugged him before he could move away from her—if he was even going to.

Sera watched her hug him for a beat too long. To his credit, he didn't touch her. Then she gathered her stuff and was gone as fast as anyone would go if they were suddenly given a day off for no reason—especially one who should've been punished.

"Did you just reward her for wearing a cocktail dress to her job?" She spun on him, so angry she could barely breathe.

"I did not. Her dress was inappropriate, so I sent her home." Harrison defended.

"She's supposed to be sent home and then has to come back, Harrison."

"That's a hassle, Seraphina." He complained to her as he folded his arms.

"That's exactly why it's done that way. So, next time, she doesn't do it. Now I will be here every week to send her home because she could come in shirtless, and you wouldn't have an issue with it." She was sure he wouldn't send her home for that, just sit and stare at her.

"I think I would notice if she came in shirtless," he argued, and his eyes dipped down to look at her chest as if *she* were shirtless.

"Of course you would notice, but you wouldn't reprimand her for it. You always make me do it, and I'm tired of always being the bad guy around here." She watched his eyes linger on her breasts then slowly come back to her eyes.

"But you're perfect for the job. A little bitchy." Harrison was looking in her eyes as he said it.

"I am not bitchy. I'm just doing my job. I will have you know that I am a very nice person when I am not doing my job." Which was completely true. At home, she relished being called bitchy. It was so rare. Not one of her kids would call her that—not ever.

"Nice girls don't take off their shirts in bars, Seraphina," Harrison said with a smarmy grin.

"What did you say?" she demanded, not denying that it happened. Sadly, that sort of thing happened often with her girls.

A few years ago, when her stepdaughter Lucy had worked for a short time at a screen-printing business, they had kept the mistakes. Sadly, Lucy had a big issue with spelling, so there were many mistakes, and the shirts were fun. From Cancan, not Cancun, to dozens that said, "Grand Cannon," they were the best shirts, and someone was always wearing a better one, so they would switch. At home or at the bar, it didn't make a difference. After all breasts were everywhere so who cared anymore?

Until someone like Harrison saw it and commented on it. What was he even doing downtown? Or had he saw it before last night? Not that him seeing her in her bra was embarrassing. It really didn't matter.

"I said girls like you don't take their shirts off in bars." His smirk got even bigger, if that was even possible. His eyes were on her breasts as he said it.

"What I do in my private life is private, Harrison. Just like yours."

"Not even going to deny it happened?" His skeptical eyes finally traveled back to hers.

"Why? You saw it happen, and it wasn't the first time, nor will it be the last. But I have never done it in this building, so there is nothing wrong with it. When it happens here, you can comment. Until then, you can forget it happened." She loved it when she could wrap a lesson into showing him it didn't embarrass her like he thought it would. Now who was the smug one?

"You are definitely a bitch, shirt on or off," he growled at her.

Yup hit a sore spot with that one.

"Harrison, you have no idea what I'm like with my shirt off. No. Clue." Sera walked out of his office as the victor of their battle of wills. Sure, she would have to spend every Friday down here talking to Kylie, but today, she'd won. Score one for Sera's team!

CHAPTER FIVE

JACKSON GRANT WAS AN ASSHOLE, a complete and utter asshole. But it seemed Harrison's date for the evening, Kendra Jones, was his friend, which was how he was now sitting across from the asshole and next to the asshole's date. His date was none other than Seraphina Lovely.

The married-with-kids, Seraphina Lovely. The bitch in HR, Seraphina. The shirtless woman from the bar just yesterday, Seraphina, all wrapped up in one woman, who wasn't having a good time on her date either.

"And my mother said, 'never mind,'" Kendra was saying to Jackson. Then she laughed, and Harrison decided whatever had come before in the conversation that he hadn't paid attention to must have been funny. Seraphina wasn't laughing, though, so maybe not.

After watching her nice ass walk out of his office earlier in the day, Harrison hadn't seen Seraphina at all until he walked into the French restaurant, Mon Amour, with Kendra. Once Kendra had seen who her date was, he insisted they join them. Harrison tried to argue that they had reservations, but Kendra wanted to eat with her friend. What a mistake that was.

So here they were, eating with the couple, and he wasn't enjoying it at all. Jackson and Kendra were talking, and neither had touched any food, while he and Seraphina were just watching and eating their salads. He was mostly eating to get this meal over with, and neither could get it over fast enough.

It seemed that since the restaurant was not far from the office, both he and Seraphina were still in what they had worn to work this morning. Though he wouldn't have changed suits for a meal, he felt that for a date, Seraphina should have stepped it up a notch—maybe not to Kylie's cocktail level, though he felt she would look amazing in a tight red dress with her breasts nearly falling out.

"So, how did you meet?" Harrison hijacked the conversation and pointed the question right at Seraphina.

"Funny story," her asshole of a date said. "We met on an app, one of those dating apps everyone's on now. This is our first date."

It wasn't even that Jackson was an asshole for hijacking his date or being on a date with a married woman—that would make *her* the asshole. It was that he was slimy as the day was long, and his story had not been the least bit funny. Harrison knew that the moment the man had called him Harry. Nobody but his mother called him that.

"First date? How's it going?" Harrison asked, getting a glimpse of Seraphina's nostrils flaring in anger. He knew all her anger ticks. This might not be the worst date ever, for him at least, but he was saving her from an asshole, so she should thank him later.

"I think it's going well, but we hadn't made it through the salad when you two arrived." Jackson was having a hard time keeping his eyes off of Kendra's breasts.

Not that Kendra's were not on display for all the world to see, but Seraphina's were bigger and currently heaving with anger. Her buttons were still buttoned to a modest level; no glimpse of what color bra she was wearing underneath.

"Do you feel it's going well also, Seraphina?" Harrison turned to her.

"I am not talking to you, Harrison," was all she said. He knew he was winning this round.

Kendra and the ass started talking about people they knew,

ignoring their dates completely. Harrison didn't mind at all; this was only his third date with Kendra, and he was really leaning towards it being the last. Sure, she was attractive, but right now, he didn't care that she was flirting with another man. And she didn't seem to care that he was watching her do it.

"No shirt change tonight?" He had to try and embarrass her about it. Even if it hadn't worked earlier in the day, maybe on her date, it would.

"Nope." She stabbed another leaf of lettuce without a hint of embarrassment, much to his disappointment.

"How does your husband feel about you dating?" he asked quietly, so the other two didn't hear.

"I'm divorced, Harrison, and have been for a few years." She leaned back in her chair and glared at him.

"I haven't heard that."

"I like to keep my personal life personal." She liked that line.

"So, what happened? Did he finally realize you were a bitch?" Harrison loved to get her worked up, and their dates were still ignoring them.

"Fuck you, Harrison," she hissed.

"You would like that, Seraphina. I'm one hell of a lay." He went there because he wanted her embarrassed. Nothing he had tried had worked yet, so he went there.

"You, Harrison, couldn't handle me in bed." Her words were so quiet that their dates couldn't hear. What the words lacked in embarrassment, they made up for in bravado.

"Is that a challenge?" He wanted to know because getting her in bed right now was what he wanted. Not only to prove her wrong but to simply have her in his bed.

"That's the truth." Folding her arms, she looked him in the eye—a direct challenge.

"And why do you think I couldn't handle you?" He leaned towards her another few inches.

"Because you haven't had sex with a *woman* in years—just girls." She nodded at his date, who was around twenty-three.

"And you're a woman?" he scoffed.

"I've done things in the bedroom that your girls have never even heard of. Hell, she may never hear of them in her lifetime," Seraphina stated and stood up.

"Sera, are you okay?" Jackson asked, tearing his eyes from Kendra's chest.

"I got a call and have to head out. It was nice to meet you," Seraphina lied to her date as she tossed money on the table.

Not waiting for a response, she turned and walked out of the restaurant, leaving him alone with the ass and his new ex-girlfriend. As usual, Seraphina had been right: Kendra was eye candy, but nothing in the bedroom. How had she even picked up on that? They had slept together twice already, and he couldn't even remember it happening.

Following her lead, he mumbled something about a call and needed to get back to the office. Neither Jackson nor Kendra mentioned it, and as the waiter came with the main course, Harrison tossed a few bills on the table and walked out the door.

Seraphina had shown him one thing tonight: Kendra wasn't what he wanted in a woman, and maybe he needed to put more effort into finding one. He wanted a woman in his bed, not a girl. Sadly, tonight, he wanted one woman in his bed, and she was a bitch.

But she wasn't married, and she wasn't seeing anyone at the moment. Maybe he had something to work with after all.

CHAPTER SIX

THE LIGHTS WERE OFF, and the house was mostly quiet when Sera walked in after her disaster of a date. She wanted to blame the entire thing on Harrison, but it was a disaster even before he'd arrived. Jackson had been a pompous jerk from the moment she sat down, not something that had come across in the messages they had sent to each other earlier in the day.

With his attitude, constant bragging about his job, and people he knew, she didn't think she would make it to the main course. Harrison walking in with a date who was barely old enough to drink had been the cherry on top. Once Harrison was around, all other men paled in comparison—always had, always would.

The TV flickered as she slipped off her heels and hung up her coat. The movie 'Twilight' was playing on the big TV in the living room, which meant someone was home. Based on the movie, it could be anyone of her girls or all of them.

"Hey, Sera," a voice called out from the depths of the plush couch. Harper.

"Hey, Mom Lovely," a deeper voice called. It was Cliff Scott, everyone's favorite bartender, which meant Lucy was there also. They were a pair, just not a couple. It was odd, but it seemed to work for them. Sera wasn't going to judge it as long as it worked for them.

"Hi, Harper, Cliff, and Lucy, I assume." She grinned at the group of twenty-something's engrossed in the teen movie.

Walking barefoot into the room, she saw Emma was there also. Her eyes were glued to the screen the same as the others, but she was an actual teen, so her concentration was expected. Ignoring her mother was also to be expected.

Stopping behind her, she kissed the top of the teen's head, her black hair smelling like a mixture of apples, sunshine, and all Emmaline. "Hey, baby, did you have a good day?"

"Yes, Mom," Emma groaned. She always reacted that way when Sera asked her.

Sera had stopped listening to the tone of the voices in her house years before Emma had hit twelve. She'd had grumpy, hormonal teens since the day she had married Bradford. Her own baby had been no different.

"Good. I'm going to make something to eat. Anyone want anything?" she called to the group, running her hand over her daughter's dark, soft hair one more time before Emma jerked her head away from her mom's hands.

She hadn't been raised with much affection and hadn't wanted that for her kids, any of them. Though she held back a little with the older girls. But she wanted her own kids to know that warmth. Her goal from day one was to show her kids that they are loved and worthy of that love. As far as she could tell, it had worked.

"Popcorn," Cliff called, and the women agreed.

"Coming up." Smiling at the group, she knew they were watching this movie because Emma was obsessed with it right now. After she had read the books, she now watched the movies over and over.

In the kitchen, she turned on the lights and started a bag of microwave popcorn for the group. Digging in the fridge, she pulled out the leftovers from a luncheon for a society wife and her friends. It was just dry chicken, but Harper was a remarkable chef, and Sera knew it would be amazing, even heated up.

Harper and Lucy were caterers and had been for a few years now. Every day their fridge was filled with leftovers from meals they'd served. The family was well fed, and the meals were amazing. Dishing up a plate, she popped it into the microwave and pulled out the bag of popped popcorn.

Harper walked into the kitchen wearing jeans and a gray "Grand Cannon" T-shirt. "How did your date go?"

"It's just after nine." Sera glanced at the clock on the wall as she dumped the popcorn into a bowl. That should say everything.

"That bad?" Harper grabbed the bowl from her as Sera snatched a handful of the stuff.

"Yup, worst. What an A-hole." Sera stuffed the handful in her mouth.

"At least you realized it right away and didn't waste too much time on him," Harper said as the microwave timer went off.

"There is at least that. Why aren't you guys not all out on the town?" Sera pointed to the group in the living room through the wall.

"Lucy was still working, so we stayed until she got here." Harper shrugged.

"And now?"

"Cliff can't leave until he knows how it ends. As if he hasn't seen it before. We might be in for the night. We just started the second one, and Cliff is all teen-girl about them." Harper complained about her sister's friend with a smile. No matter what, Cliff was liked by all the Lovelys.

"We have enough alcohol for a Twilight party," Sera replied, knowing she was probably right about Cliff. The same thing had happened with Harry Potter; he had stayed for days on that one.

"I think I'll get something for me, but those lazies will have to get their own." Harper put the bowl down and headed for the basement.

Taking her plate from the microwave, Sera regretted that she hadn't heated it in the oven, but that took way more time. Sera was ready for this week to be done, so waiting for a plate of food to heat was beyond her now.

She was half done with her chicken before Harper came back up the stairs, loaded down with bottles of booze. Wine, beer, wine coolers, and a bottle of something hard.

"Are you inviting more people over?" Sera asked, looking at her oldest daughter's haul as she set them carefully on the counter, then made sure that they were all standing.

"No, why?" she asked, pushing the bottles further onto the counter.

"No reason." Sera hid her smile.

Harper took the popcorn and two wine coolers, then headed into the living room, telling those in the room about the booze as she went. Within moments, Lucy and Cliff were in the kitchen in their matching gray Grand Cannon T-shirts and shorts. Cliff took two beers and headed back to the movie, not wanting to miss anything.

Lucy stayed behind and opened the bottle of wine, taking out a tall water glass that had a Disney princess on it, and she poured herself a generous amount. "Want some?"

"Sure," Sera said and watched her daughter do the same for her. The bottle was almost empty after the two glasses were full.

"I gave you a little more … shitty date and all." Lucy grinned and picked up the one with less in it, though Sera could barely tell the difference.

"Thanks, Luce," Sera said to the brunette as she went back to her movie.

Putting her empty plate in the dishwasher, she grabbed two Cokes from the fridge and grabbed her wine in the other hand. Heading out to the living room, she gave one of the pops to Emma, who barely noticed her but did grab the beverage. Fighting the urge to kiss her head, Sera instead headed for her room.

Upstairs, she dropped off her wine on her nightstand, and headed up to the third floor. Agatha would be drawing; it was a given. Even though her daughter hadn't made a lick of money on her talent, she didn't stop doing it. Drawing was her only constant. Jobs came and went but drawing remained.

"Everyone is downstairs watching Twilight," Sera told her as she crested the top of the stairs and saw her hard at work, with a half-sleeping seven-year-old watching from a chair nearby.

"They are so fucking lucky." Agatha looked up at her with a grin. *No way was this one going down to watch that movie series,* Sera thought to herself. Sera wasn't even sure she had made it through the first of the movies back when the obsession first hit the house.

"Just saying." Sera laughed and set the other pop on her easel.

Agatha was the second to the youngest and was completely different than her sisters. She was the first of Bradford's children she suspected wasn't actually Bradford's. Buzz the baby was also not his, with her red hair and gray-brown eyes. Judith Lovely would've have had a lot of explaining to do if she had stuck around.

Oddly, it was her first black-haired daughter that called her mom. None of the others did on a regular basis. Mostly just in love or sarcasm, or both. But she and Agatha had a bond that she didn't have with the others. It was more than just their shared love of the girls, and it went beyond friendship. The twenty-six-year-old was probably her daughter in every way but birth at this point.

"You're home from your date early. I thought you would be out until morning." Agatha leaned back in her chair. In the last few months, the attic dweller had finally gained a pound or two. She was even looking healthy—not happy, but healthy.

"Not tonight. A dud." Sera picked up the half-asleep little girl from the old green chair and sat down with her on her lap.

This one had black-haired as well. At seven, she was still Sera's baby. Violet was Agatha's shadow and wanted more than anything to be Agatha, but her personality was her mom's, and everyone knew that. Bubbly and outgoing was something Agatha would never be.

Agatha cracked open the can of pop. "Too bad."

"Do you work tonight?" Sera asked. You never knew with Agatha; she worked nights and got fired more often than not.

"Yes, Cliff got me on at the Grog until this shit blows over. So much for his 'never going to work here again' speech of last winter. What an ass. Tips are big right now, though." Agatha shrugged. Bartending was never going to be Agatha's thing, but she kept at it for now. She was always complaining and usually got fired after a few weeks ... or days ... or hours.

"I was in there last night. It was insane for a Thursday." She didn't mention that Harrison had been in there or that he had seen her topless. Or that he mentioned it twice now and was trying to rattle her.

"It is, and I hate it. Where do we go now that the Grog's been stolen by hipsters? I can't drink with a hipster." Agatha moaned. It was their bar, but if they were going to meet at a bar, it was the Grog.

"It'll die down once everyone realizes it's a dive." Sera noticed her baby had fallen asleep in her arms.

"I hope so." Agatha was looking at the girl also. The nineteen-year age difference on them was nothing, based on how close the two were.

More often than not, people assumed that Agatha was Violet's mother since they shared their hair color and artistic talent. Sera was the complete opposite and had no artistic talent at all.

"I better put her to bed." Sera looked down at Violet, who was already in yellow pajamas, thanks to her older sister.

Sera tried not to take advantage of Agatha or any of her adult daughters, but sometimes it was nice knowing that she didn't have to worry about her kids getting home on time or getting them places. Being a single mother was stressful enough, but she had so much less stress because of the girls.

"You do that. I'll be up here until eleven, and then I work until close," Agatha said. She always worked nights, always.

When Bradford kept putting off his return date until he didn't even pretend anymore, the five girls had been there when Emmaline had been born. They'd also been there when she needed someone to watch the baby, so she could continue with school. It had even been Harper who had insisted that Sera start dating after Emma had been born since Bradford was living with a woman anyway.

During her ten-year marriage, she had only spent a total of three weeks with her husband and had never shared a bed or even wanted to. He had married her for his kids, and she had married him for hers. In the end, she got them all and loved them to bits.

It seemed that they liked her also since they all still lived at home. All seven of her girls were under one roof at the same time almost every night. It was a good thing that Bradford had bought a large old house when he and his first wife Judith started to have kids. The six-bedroom house was full, with Agatha in the attic and Buzz on the couch right now. They were still apt to stay over at a boyfriend's or just a male friend at any time, but it had always seen that way.

Sera didn't want to put Violet in her own room tonight, so she took her to bed with her. Tonight, she needed the closeness of her daughter's body to hers.

After stripping out of her work clothes, she pulled on a pale green "Bastan" shirt and matching yellow shorts. Dimming the lights in the room, she climbed in beside her little girl and took a sip of wine as she looked over the most adorable little thing around. Not that Emma wasn't just as cute, but the surly teen's attitude got in the way sometimes.

Like Emma, Violet had the most beautiful blue eyes Sera had ever seen. Each had inherited that from their father, a father that they shared by sheer chance. A father that had no idea he was even a father at all.

Not that she had intentionally not told him about Emma. She had only known his first name and hadn't seen him for years after it happened. Once she had finally known his last name, he was already happily married. At least then, he was.

During a low point in his marriage and a drunken Christmas party a few years later, they had hooked up again. This time, it seemed the condom had broken, and she got Violet while he remained married for another few years. At the time, she had been married as well.

Not one moment had Sera regretted that drunken interaction that had given her the baby. She was the baby of the house, and always had been.

It had been easy to not tell Harrison he was a father; he couldn't remember her from college, nor what had happened at that party. So far, he had said nothing about either one, so she assumed he didn't remember her and couldn't remember that night. But man, she did ... often.

Running a hand over her baby's hair, she didn't regret not telling him. She didn't want to share her kids with anyone. They were hers, and Harrison Dean would never know about them. He may not like her or do anything but piss her off at work, but when she got home, it was his eyes that their daughters had and his hair she got to caress. His babies that she got to love when she couldn't love him.

CHAPTER SEVEN

SO FAR, he hadn't seen Seraphina at all this week. Maybe it was because Kylie hadn't shown up for work yet to get in trouble. On Monday, he had thought she just forgot to call in, but by today, he had to call Seraphina and tell her that his secretary was a no-show again. Two days was too many.

Not that he didn't want to talk to Seraphina; he very much did. But he knew he couldn't talk to her about what he wanted to talk to her about at work, which was sex, and why she thought she was so good at it. He knew for a fact she wasn't—well, not for a fact since he had never slept with the woman. But he knew the cold, bitchy type, and they were never good in bed.

There was a sharp rap on his door frame, making him look up at the woman on his mind. In her serious voice, she stated, "Conference room, now."

Now, if Kylie had been there, she would have announced Seraphina instead of letting her scare him while he was thinking about her and sex. Or maybe not … Kylie wasn't that good at her job.

Getting up, he followed her, enjoying the look of her ass in the black skirt and long legs that were below it. Had she always been this tall? Most likely.

Seraphina shut the door behind him as he entered. They were alone in the room. Not that they hadn't spent many battles alone in rooms, but they didn't usually start out alone. Or maybe they did. They'd had so many fights, the protocol was probably not as strong as he was thinking.

"Sit down. We have to talk." She wasn't smiling for the first time in years as she pointed at the table with a blue file in her hand. He had noticed over the years she never used manila ones, always colored ones. But if there was a pattern, he hadn't figured it out yet.

"Okay, darling." He teased her, but he really didn't know why.

"Don't fuck with me this morning." Taking the seat across the table, she glared at him.

"Haven't we already discussed this, Seraphina?" He leaned back in his chair, eyes on her perfect breasts under her white shirt. No heaving. She wasn't mad yet.

Having her call him into a room for a fight was even better then talking to her about sex. This way, he could think about sex as her breasts heaved, and she lost her cool.

"Be serious, Harrison. Now, have you seen Kylie Nash this week?" she demanded. Couldn't she have just asked in his office?

He grinned. "No, she hasn't called in. I was going to call you today."

"Did you see or speak to her since you sent her home on Friday?" she asked, opening the file and looking in it.

"No, I went on a date on Friday, and you were there. I didn't do much else this weekend," he replied, wondering what was happening. He didn't want to go into detail about what he did on his time off—it wasn't any of her business. It was also as boring as laundry and sports on TV.

"How long have you known her?" He watched as she wrote down his answers.

"Two or three months." He sat up straight. Where was she going with these questions?

"Can you be more exact?"

"No, I don't remember at all. She's just my personal assistant. You can look in your records."

"How long have you been sleeping with her?"

"I have never slept with her. She's twenty, for Christ's sake." He finally admitted the truth to her. Her attitude wasn't improving with his teasing, and his was taking a turn for the worse because of it.

"She claims you've been sleeping with her since she started working here and that the baby she's carrying is yours. She's filed a paternity case against you and a harassment lawsuit against you and Rodgers and Associates."

The room lost focus for a moment as her words settled in. He was being sued, and by Kylie Nash of all people, the girl who just last week tried to get into his pants. She had been like that since day one. Some days, he enjoyed the attention, but it had gotten old over the last month.

"I have never slept with her or even tried," he stated.

"Conference room," Seraphina said the two words and pointed at the table they were currently sitting at. It had only been last week when that had happened.

"Nothing happened. She tried to get into my pants. I've told her I have a girlfriend over and over." He groaned, now wishing he hadn't tried to make Sera angry and just said nothing happened then.

"Why would she do this then?"

"I have no idea. She maybe wants to marry me. I don't fucking know," he rambled.

"So, the baby isn't yours?" she asked as she wrote things in her file, her eyes not lifting to his.

"No fucking way. Even if I had slept with her, I have slow swimmers. You can ask my ex about those things. I can't father kids, ever. Write *that* down." He waved his hand at her because she stopped writing as he'd talked. Her blue eyes were on him instead of the paper.

"You're sure?" she choked out.

"One-hundred percent. Doctors checked many times while I was married. No baby Deans out there anywhere. Not now, not ever, and not in that woman." Harrison suddenly pounded the table in anger. He hated talking about it; it made him feel like less of a man, but he needed it out there that Kylie Nash was a lying bitch.

"I don't care if the child is yours or not. She claims it was conceived in this office building, and I care about that. So, did you ever sleep with her? Drunk or sober?"

"No, never. I don't drink enough to get blind drunk anymore. Those days are behind me." He wished he'd never had any, but his divorce had been a shitshow, and drinking dulled that. His divorce had lasted more years than he should have let it go on. At the time, he wasn't willing to let go of what they had; what they could have had. Was it all for a dream? He didn't know anymore.

"I'll contact her lawyer. At this point, I think we have to demand a paternity test. If it comes back as yours, I'll be pissed." Seraphina slammed her folder closed.

"Not as pissed as I will be since I didn't touch her," he hissed.

"Once we get the test back, and it's negative, it's possible that she will back down." Sera tapped the folder.

"I told her I had a girlfriend the entire time, not that she cared. She just kept pushing. Now I see what she had planned," Harrison said.

"I would suggest you hang on to that girlfriend through this process. It'll be helpful to parade her in front of a judge if need be." Sera wasn't looking at him as she said the words. She was looking out the window at the city.

"That won't be possible because I haven't had one the entire time, and the one I had last week is over," he admitted, two days too soon, it seemed.

"Kendra? But you were just out with her." Her eyes went back to him in surprise.

"And she spent more time flirting with your date than talking to me. So, I ended it. Not long after you left the restaurant." No way was he admitting he got the idea from her.

"Can you get her back?"

"I don't want her back."

"I would suggest you find a replacement pronto."

"Pronto?" He cracked a smile for the first time since the woman started talking.

"Right away, Harrison." Her big blue eyes were on him.

"I know what it means, Seraphina. I just haven't heard anyone say it in years."

Her eyes squinted at him, but not in anger. She never did that in anger.

"Are we done here?"

"Yes, we are. I don't think I need to tell you to keep this confidential, do I?" she asked.

"No way am I telling anyone. Are you going out to the bar tonight?" he asked, not knowing why. He didn't actually care, but he was getting drunk tonight—that was for sure.

She tapped her folder again. "No, the bar's full of yuppies now."

"You only go to one bar?" he asked in amazement.

"No." She grinned. "I go to others. I just like that bar. Also, it's Tuesday, and I have to work tomorrow."

"The last time I saw you there was a Thursday. You worked the next day."

"Well, I had a shitty day that day, so I needed a drink."

"Maybe today could turn out shitty."

"It might just get there since you failed to inform me about Nash not showing up for work this week. I might have not been so shocked when I got the legal paperwork on this." Seraphina got up and grabbed her folder. "Next time, just tell me when an employee doesn't show up."

"I'll get right on that. when it happens." He watched her walk out of the room.

As the door shut behind her, he wondered what she was thinking. Just last week, he had let her believe that he'd had sex in a conference room with Kylie. Now he was claiming he had never touched her. Now he regretted playing with Seraphina about the relationship. He had only admitted it because it would rile her up. And it had worked, until now.

CHAPTER EIGHT

TUCKING her toes under her butt on her chair, Sera looked over the document that had just come across her fax machine. Nine years ago, Dr. Liven had stated that Harrison Dean indeed had sluggish sperm. The words were right there on the page in front of her.

She hadn't actually expected to see this document at all. After telling him that Kylie Nash had agreed to take the paternity test, she fully expected him to admit that he lied to her. Or at least lied to her yesterday because she was sure he hadn't lied to her last Friday.

It didn't matter what the paper she was holding said; she knew he could father children. Though her first could easily be dismissed as happening before whatever happened to his reproductive ability, Violet had been conceived after this test was conducted—almost a year later.

Sera knew the girl was his. At the time, she hadn't had sex in the four months preceding the conception or in the year after. Months before, she had broken up with a longtime boyfriend who had wanted her to move in with him. The relationship had ended because he was mad that she had said no. At the time, she needed her older girls to help out with Emma, who was seven at the time. Also, he wanted her to leave behind Buzz and Agatha, who were in high school, arguing that Lucy and Mabel were living there and were adults. At twenty, they were barely adults. Besides, no man was separating her from her kids.

After the breakup, she had laid low for months, concentrating on the girls and getting them through school. But the night of the Christmas party, she had let herself go—not something she usually did.

They had both been very drunk, but he'd been worse than her. She didn't remember who had started kissing who, but both had been willing when they'd gotten to his office. An hour or so later, she had walked out, and he had passed out.

There was no denying that the baby born nine months later was his. She was the spitting image of her sister and her dad. No paternity tests were needed with her two.

At the time of Violet's birth, he had still been married to Veronica, and she had still been married to Bradford, who she remained married to for another year until Buzz graduated from high school. No way was she divorcing him, knowing any of the bigger girls could end up in foster care.

In the years following his divorce, Harrison had treated Seraphina like he hated her, so she kept her information to herself. His marriage had hung on for years, on and off at any moment. Sera didn't even know that the marriage was completely over for months after it had actually happened. Even with him being single, she never let on that she kept a piece or two of him home with her every day.

So, whether he was counting on the fact that he was shooting blanks on his paternity test wasn't known yet. If he was counting on a negative result to clear his name, he was in for a problem if the kid was his.

Setting aside the test results, she tried to put her involvement in Harrison's life out of her mind. This had nothing to do with her, nothing at all. They weren't even friends at this point, just co-workers —co-workers with a past that only one of them remembered.

Picking up her phone, she shot a quick text to Agatha to say she was working late tonight. Agatha didn't care when Sera came home; she would keep the little girl forever if need be.

She set her phone aside again and went back to what she was doing: performance reviews. Yes, it was that time of the year again. Most companies no longer did the tedious task anymore, but Rodgers and Associates was still hanging on to the practice. And she was lucky enough to have to go through them every time.

After an hour, she was bored out of her mind. Spinning in her chair, she looked out the window and wondered if any of the girls were out tonight. But she knew the answer was no. Even though it was Wednesday, she knew that Lucy and Harper were working on a catering job, and Agatha was home with Violet. Maby never went out without her sisters, and Buzz had just started her career as a reporter and was working tonight.

Things were really changing for the family. All her restless girls were settling into careers. Only Maby had ever wanted to go to college; Buzz had because she was smart and hadn't thought of anything else to do.

Even with having a baby, she had made it through college in the standard four years. Getting on at Rodgers and Associates in HR had been a dream come true, only to be surprised when she had been hired as the director not long after Violet had been born.

But Bradford's girls were different; they had been since the beginning. They were artistic and outgoing. Never were they going to follow the path set out for them; they would all forge their own way through life. And she was going to sit back and watch it happen. There was no way she could have told any of them to be caterers or reporters or even a teacher—that was all them.

"I figured you would be out on a date tonight," Harrison said from behind her. Of course, she knew it was him. She could feel him in the room.

Spinning back to her desk, she said, "Not tonight. Performance reviews. I like to get them done as soon as possible."

"Doesn't look like you're getting any done." He chuckled at her.

"I was taking a break. I am allowed, you know." She crossed her arms as she spoke. He always tried to get her riled up.

"Did you get the document from my doctor?" Harrison moved into the room and sat in the chair across from her.

"Yes, but I don't think it really matters until we get the paternity test. That will tell us for sure you aren't the father."

"I know for certain I'm not the father because I didn't have sex with her."

"That's not what you said a week ago," she pointed out.

"A week ago, I was fucking with you, Seraphina!"

"Well, don't ever fuck with me, Harrison. I deserve respect from you and from every lawyer here who thinks I'm not worth anything because I didn't go to law school." Okay, so she went a little over-board, but she got tired of being the bad guy every day around here.

"I don't think of it that way, I swear. I'm sorry if I ever made you feel less because you're not a lawyer." He seemed sincere, but some-times he did when he was fucking with her.

"Thank you, Harrison. Now, what do you want?" Yes, she knew she was being short with him, but it was after hours, and she didn't want to deal with him.

"Just to see if you have heard anything more on Kylie?"

"So far, I know that she can't get the paternity test done for another two weeks. Then it will take a few days to a week to get the results back. If you are telling the truth, this will all be over in less than a month. But if you are lying, I don't know what's going to happen. There's no way to prove whether she was a willing participant or not. Or even if it was conceived in the office." Sera hated talking about this.

"I have never had sex in this building, and the kid is not mine." He leaned back in his chair with confidence she herself didn't feel. She knew for a fact that he had sex in this building ... with her.

"I hope so, Harrison, because I've had your back on this, and if you have lied to me, I will never trust you again," she said truthfully.

He rubbed his hands over his face. "I never touched that woman. I don't even know why she's going through all this."

"I wish I knew also," she replied as a text came in, and she glanced at her phone. She was getting texts from the girls about meeting up in a few hours.

Harrison glanced at the phone that was dinging at a steady rate. "You suddenly got popular."

"Just a group text." She grabbed it and shut off the sound. It seemed that the girls were going out again tonight, but she wasn't going to this time.

"You can answer it. It's after hours." He looked at it again.

"No, they'll be okay. I have to get these reports done." She picked up one to show that she was going to do it, but she was really done for the day. She hated the reports.

"See you later then," Harrison said but didn't move.

"I'll call you as soon as I know anything else," she answered as her phone buzzed on the desk again.

His eyes were on it as he backed away from her office. In disappointment, she watched him go, wishing he had turned around. He had a nice butt, and she could use a glimpse of it tonight.

CHAPTER NINE

THURSDAY MORNING HAD Harrison sitting in Keith Davidson's office, getting a lecture on proper office conduct. Yes, from a man who had gotten not one but three secretaries pregnant over the years. Two he married, and one has not been seen since but is rumored to still have a relationship with her former boss.

Harrison had let the older man's words roll off his back until Seraphina's name crossed his lips. "Sera Lovely is performing a small in-house investigation. She will be talking to you and others. I want this taken care of yesterday."

"There's nothing for a report, Keith. I didn't sleep with her in the office or out of it, and I never suggested I wanted to," Harrison stated. At this point, he was tired of the entire thing, and it hadn't even been a week since he had learned about it.

"I hope not, Harrison. Women these days." Keith's words betrayed his feelings about the subject, even after a lecture that said the opposite.

"If that's everything, I have work to do." He wanted out of this office. Keith had never been his friend, and they were never going to be.

"Go. Sera will tell me when she finds out anything," Keith replied.

Leaving his boss's office, he wondered how his life had come to the moment when Keith Davidson seemed like a good guy, and he looked like the jerk. At this point, he was in limbo about the entire thing. Nobody would believe him until the results came back, but that was going to take weeks—weeks he didn't want to waste convincing people he didn't have sex with a twenty-year-old at work.

But he still had no idea how he was going to prove it didn't happen. The only proof would be his constant denial, and he had messed that up by bragging to the one woman who mattered in this: the one doing the investigating.

Stopping in her office last night had not been reassuring. Even with the report, she was skeptical that the kid wasn't his. He could have sent her five of those same reports that all said the same thing. It was a fact he had learned to accept years before. Now everyone in the company would know; that stuff always seemed to leak out.

Deciding he had better just talk to Seraphina about the investigation instead of it distracting him all day, he headed towards her office again. For almost a week now, he hadn't been able to get her out of his mind. But it was the investigation that was taking him to her office now, not the woman herself. Or the constant urge to talk to her suddenly.

Today she was hard at work and not looking out the window. No toes peeking out from under her butt on her chair. Just a smile and dedication on her face today.

"So, you're heading up my investigation?" he questioned her from the doorway.

Her blonde head snapped up, and her blue eyes locked on him. "I tried to tell Keith that we shouldn't be investigating it ourselves. We need outside council for that, but Keith isn't exactly known for his good judgment."

Smiling at her words, he walked into the office, wondering if she was barefoot under the desk like Friday night. "Are we talking about the same Keith I know? The one with four ex-wives and two baby mamas?"

"One and the same. Can you shut the door? I need to talk to you."

Her words surprised him. He wasn't expecting her to have any information yet. Maybe he shouldn't have stopped if it was going to be this quick.

Shutting the door, he stayed by it, "What do you need?"

"Harrison ..." She leaned back in her chair, pen now resting on the desk. "I do not want to conduct an investigation into your conduct. The lawsuit into the paternity part of the case is off my desk; the test will be the answer. I'm looking into the harassment part of the claim."

"Okay, what does that mean?" Harrison walked to the chair across from her desk. He could tell she wasn't excited to do this task.

"It means that I'll have to ask you some probably embarrassing questions and that you need to be truthful, even if it is embarrassing. Did you want a man present for an interview? Another woman?" She leaned forward again.

"No one else is needed. If you can't handle what I say, that's on you." He sank into the chair, not taking his eyes off her.

"I can handle anything that comes my way, Harrison."

"Good. Did you want to do it now or later?" she asked, starting to gather up the papers on her desk.

"Now works. Get it done with." His eyes were on her as she organized and filed the papers in her desk, bringing out a green file.

"Okay, let's start with the basics. How long have you been with the company?"

"Ten years, and you?" Harrison asked. Had she been there when he had been hired?

"This isn't about me," she shot back.

"It might be easier if we can make it more of a chat than an interview." Harrison countered. He really didn't think she would answer.

"Twelve next summer. How long were you married, and when did you get a divorce?"

"Married since I was twenty and divorced for four years. And you?" He liked this so far.

"Married at nineteen and divorced for six. Did you cheat on your spouse?"

"Yes, a few times in the end. The divorce was very drawn out, and she was already living with the man she married later when I did. And you?" He knew she wouldn't answer this one. The rest had been easy.

"Yes. Have you ever had an affair with someone at work?" She went on as if she didn't just admit to cheating on her husband. He wished she would elaborate—she didn't seem the type to cheat.

"No, I haven't. I knew that it would never go anywhere, and I would have to continue working with the woman. I'm not getting remarried again. One and done. You?"

"Yes. Have you ever touched anyone inappropriately at the office that you are aware of?" She went on once again like her answer wasn't a complete shock to him.

"No, I have not. Okay, back to your answer. Yes, that you don't want to get married again, or yes, you had an affair with someone at the office?" He leaned forward in his chair. Her pen had stopped.

"Both, actually. Can you answer the question?"

"Who?" He had never heard a whisper about it, ever.

"This isn't about me, Harrison. Can you answer the question?" she stated again.

"I did, Seraphina. I said no." He had flustered her. It was cute because she was actually getting red, though it wasn't as satisfying as he had thought it would be.

"Did you ever date Kylie Nash?" she asked him again.

"No, I have never seen her outside of this building." He answered her question and watched her write.

"Did you ever touch Kylie Nash inappropriately?"

"No. She touched me on occasion, but I distracted her."

She looked up from her paper. "How?"

"By ignoring her verbal advances, pushing her away, and stating I have a girlfriend."

"Did you?"

"Sometimes, but usually not. I am not a purvey old man, and she was young. Have you ever slept with someone who was twenty?"

Her eyes found his again. "I don't know. I don't have them fill out a questionnaire," she quipped. "Why do you think Kylie Nash is doing this to you?"

"I don't know. I don't have the kind of money other lawyers in the firm have, or the loose scruples they have either. If she would have picked over a dozen guys here, they would have happily put her up in an apartment and given her anything she wanted. But I'm not like that." He leaned back in his chair.

"Do you have family money she thinks she can get a hold of?" Sera asked.

"No, I came from nothing. My ex's family had money, but I was raised by a single mom who scraped by to get me through school," he admitted. Not many people know that he came from nothing.

"Where is your mom now? Are you still in contact with her?" Sera asked.

"I bought her a little place my second year out of school. She's now retired and loves to garden and can finally dedicate her time to art," he said, happy with his decision to take care of the woman who had taken care of him for all those years. She deserved more than he could give her, and he gave her everything he could.

Her eyes snapped up to his at his last word. "What kind of art?"

"Oils mostly. She does landscapes. Sells some, but not much yet." He was interested in her interest in his mom. Most women didn't care about her, not even his ex.

"What's her name?" She was no longer pretending to write it down.

"Emily Dean. Her work is under E Dean. Do you know her?" he asked since her eyes went wide when he said her name.

"No, just sounds familiar, that's all," her voice cracked, and she turned her attention quickly back to her papers on her desk.

Letting go of the odd reaction, he asked, "Why green?"

She shook her head as if to clear it. "What?"

"Your folder is green today. I never see you with green." He leaned over and taped the tiny bit he could see.

"Green is for senior partners. Complaints and requests," she admitted. He had thought it was all random.

"Why not manila?"

"They're boring. I like color in my life," she said as if she didn't always wear the same drab colors. He couldn't remember her wearing any other color except in the bar that night.

"Are we done here?" he asked.

"Yes, for now. I have to interview Kylie Nash at some point. I have decided to talk to Aspen Andrews. Do you think Kylie will have an issue with her?"

"I don't think so. I don't even know if they know each other. Why her?"

"She's leaving in two weeks, so she has as close to no interest in the case as I can get. Do you know her?"

"Not really. She's a personal lawyer; I'm corporate." He had heard the name but couldn't put a face on it.

"Okay, please stay away from her … and Kylie, if you actually see her," Seraphina stated as he got up from the chair.

"Don't worry. I will."

"Good. I think I'm done with you for a while. I have more interviews today and tomorrow about this." Her smile was dimmed today, and he missed it.

"Have fun with that," he said as he walked out the door.

CHAPTER TEN

SHE OPENED the green file one more time and looked at the name that popped out at her as if she had to see it again to remember it. Emily Dean, so close to her own Emmaline that it shocked her upon hearing it.

When her Emma had been born, she was waffling between Grace and Abigail and was waiting to see the baby to decide. But upon seeing the little red baby with her black hair and her already deep blue eyes, the name Emmaline had popped into her head. And since she was very emotional and had no one to say no to it, she had went with it.

Even after all these years, Sera still loved her first baby's name and wouldn't change it for anything. And now her name so closely mirrored her grandma's, and Sera was feeling the guilt over it more and more.

Should she have told him about the girls? But what would she say? How do you tell a man you have known and had hundreds of conversations with that he fathered your child in college? That you knew she was his the moment he started working for the company you both work at. And do you also share that though he had no memory of it, he had had sex at the office at least once? That he had cheated on his wife years before he thought he had? And that she had proof that all the tests he had taken were incorrect? Violet was her proof.

Violet, her little artist. For years she had assumed the art had come as a side effect of being around Agatha all the time. Agatha was the artist. Now Sera knew that her baby had gotten the art gene from Harrison's mom. Sera was raising another wild and crazy artist.

After an hour of searching for Emily Dean on the internet, Sera came up empty. As far as she could find, the woman was not on the internet with her work or with social media, so she had no idea what her kid's grandma looked like as her first interview of the day started.

By 5 p.m., she had conflicting reports from people who work with Harrison. On one hand, he was hard-working, and nobody ever saw anything untoward happen. On the other, he bragged about his out-of-office conquests to those he deemed friends, but none said he ever talked about in-office romances, if there were any to talk about.

But tomorrow, she was talking to Kylie Nash, and she was the one who would know what really happened. Or she would lie to her, and Sera wouldn't put it past her to lie.

It seemed Kylie kept to herself and hadn't made any friends at work. It had either been a lonely three months, or her friends had quickly abandoned her when she left. Either way, she had to find out the truth, and soon.

But tonight, she wasn't staying late—she was going home to see her kids. They had been on her mind all day, and she just wanted to hug them and know that they were real. Some days were like that lately, as if Harrison not knowing about them made them less real to her, which was crazy; they were a part of her every day.

"Lost in thought again, Seraphina?" Harrison asked from the door.

Snapping herself from her thoughts, she looked at him. He was a good looking as always. It wasn't his day that had been spent discussing someone else's sex life in detail. Too much detail. That was her.

"Sorry, yes. Just thinking about life."

"Don't go so deep, Seraphina," he said with a grin.

"Can you possibly call me Sera?" She hated her given name, and he was the only person who used it … except her girls when they were teasing her or mad at her … or both.

"I can try, but it won't be easy," Harrison replied, leaning against the door jam.

"Just try, please, or I'll call you Harry." She turned to clean off her desk for the day. It was after five now.

"Nobody calls me Harry, ever." His smile was gone.

"Diddo, Harry." She locked her file cabinet as she said it.

"Okay, I'll try harder tomorrow." He stood up straight. "Walk you out?"

His words took her by surprise—what was he trying to do? Was he trying to influence her investigation? He had never spent so much time with her.

"Sure, I guess," she said and walked with him to the elevator, where they waited with half a dozen others.

At ground level, he walked with her as she headed to the parking lot where her car was. She never parked in the underground parking, ever, preferring to pay more to park in a lot down the street.

"Do you always park out here?" he asked in surprise.

"Yes, I just like to go outside at the end of the day," she lied. No way was she telling him her true reason.

"Some days aren't nice," he said of the snowy cold winters they got.

"Some days are. Here I am." She pointed to the red, late-model Jeep she drove. Yes, she could afford a new one, but this one was still running, so she kept it.

"A classic jeep? I didn't see that from you."

"And what should I be driving?"

"A high-end sedan in gray." He laughed.

"Nope. I was raised a Jeep girl, and there's no changing that now." Her dad hadn't left a big imprint on her after all these years, but he had been a Jeep man.

"You do surprise me, Sera. See? I did it." He grinned like he had achieved a big goal.

"I will see you tomorrow, Harrison." She opened the door of the Jeep.

"Maybe my name will be clear then." His eyes were on her legs as she climbed into the vehicle.

"Maybe," she replied and pulled the door shut.

Backing out of the parking stall, Harrison just stood and watched her. She still didn't know why he had walked her to her car, but she liked that he had.

CHAPTER ELEVEN

YESTERDAY SERAPHINA HAD BEEN out of the office for the entire day. Harrison had heard through the grapevine that she was interviewing Kylie Nash in the morning but hadn't heard why she would be out the entire day. Aspen Andrews was back by lunch.

Maybe he was naive to think his shorter interview was the norm. Since she already had an opinion about it him, it wasn't hard to figure out why she would make the interview short.

Even if his interview had been short, he had learned so much about the woman he thought he knew. Their lives seemed to mirror each other in that they married young and stayed married for a lot of years. Both marriages seemed to have ended badly. Though her answers were short, they were telling.

But what nagged him was her sleeping with someone at the office. She had been there for a long time and had admitted to cheating on her ex, so it could have been anytime during the twelve years she had been there. And it could have been with anyone from the mailroom to the partners' offices. Did they meet here or outside of work?

Spinning in his chair, he headed to her office to see if she would update him on his case after all the interviews she had conducted.

Maybe she had more than Kylie to speak to yesterday, but then why send Aspen back to the office alone?

From down the hallway, he saw her door was open, so he headed down to see her. At her doorway, he saw her blonde head bent over a file on her desk. Even from the door, he could see it was yellow. Her pen was busy writing, then she stopped suddenly, tossed down her pen, and started typing on the computer.

Rapping his knuckles on the doorframe, her head snapped up and looked at him in question. He could tell she didn't want anyone to disturb her.

"You're in today." The words were out of his mouth before he could stop them. It was a stupid thing to say.

But she just grinned. "Yes, all day. Yesterday I had some things to take care of out of the office."

Harrison walked into the room since she seemed like she was in a good mood. "How did the interview go?"

"Sorry, Harrison, but I can't talk about that with you." Her smile dimmed slightly.

He tried not to be mad at her since it was her job. But for some reason, he wanted her to believe him.

"Okay. How was your day then?"

"Just an afternoon with friends. One had a birthday, so we went out to celebrate." She shrugged.

"Are you hungover, Sera?" He asked with a grin. She didn't look like it.

"No, Harrison, I'm not." She was actually smiling back at him. "I was yesterday."

"Were you able to stay dressed during your night out?" He wanted to see if he could embarrass her about it.

"I can't remember," she answered. Not even a hint of embarrassment from her.

"Must have been a good night."

"It was." Still, she didn't go into it, though it seemed like she wanted to. "But I need to get these progress reports done."

With that, he was dismissed for the day. No more details about her night of drinking or about her findings the day before. He got up and walked out without saying goodbye, which was okay since she didn't either. The bitch from HR was back.

Back in his office, he sat down in his chair, stared out his window, and tried to think about something other than Sera Lovely. Except all he could think about was her out on the town so drunk, she couldn't remember what happened the next day. It seemed so out of character; the woman he thought he knew wasn't who she really was.

Was it possible that the real Sera Lovely was the one in the bar, the one willing to take her shirt off? Not the one that was following and enforcing rules every day here?

Could he have known her for years and not have known her at all?

Was he just now learning who she actually was?

Was he liking her more and more the more he learned about her, the more she let him in?

CHAPTER TWELVE

THE ENTIRE OFFICE was dark when Sera finally pulled herself away from the reports. Though she was close to done with them, her mind was done for the day. Taking Thursday off had been a mistake when she looked at her work piled up. It had been a bad idea, except she had loved every minute of it after the interview.

But there had been no way she was dragging herself in to do these reports after getting home from the bar at 7 a.m. Bars close way before that, unless your daughter is a bartender who doesn't think rules apply to her. Or, more importantly, when everyone's favorite bartender let them stay all night.

So, there was only one option, and that was calling in sick, then proceeding to actually spend most of the day sick. It had been years since she had been that hungover.

But the day had been spent with her four less responsible girls fighting for space on the couch and using the three bathrooms in the house. She had mostly lost the couch battle but had her own bathroom in her bedroom, so she let the others have the two more public bathrooms.

The reason she had drunk so much? Kylie Nash. Even Aspen hadn't known if the woman was lying or not. If she was, she was very skilled in it because she acted innocent as hell. All big eyes and tears over what had happened. The empty promises and oh-so-heated exchanges.

Walking into the little apartment Kylie shared with her mom, Sera was struck by the fact that this could have been her, her and Emma. If she hadn't made the mistake of marrying Bradford, she would have had to raise her alone, with possibly two years of college and nothing more.

A little two-bedroom on the second floor with little room to stretch out and even less privacy. Sera knew she wouldn't have made it past entry-level jobs as she left her child with strangers just to work long hours.

After talking to the twenty-year-old, Sera had known that her dislike of Kylie was still evident and hadn't improved because she had tried to hurt Harrison. He wasn't hers, but she was starting to think of him as someone she needed to protect.

Her answers to the questions were in complete opposition of what Harrison had said. According to Kylie, the entire affair—a month's long one—had taken place completely at the office. Not once had they met up after work; he had a girlfriend, and he didn't want her to know about his office fling. It had ended right after Sera, herself, had talked to him about the conference room sex—which for sure happened, according to Kylie.

Harrison had denied it all; every fact that Kylie had laid out had been contradicted by him already. Sera had wondered if he would change his story, but since the beginning, he had stuck to the same one. She knew she would have to conduct another interview with him but was putting it off a week or so in case his story changed again.

What had made Sera question Kylie's story, one she hadn't told Aspen about, was that according to Kylie, they always had sex on the desk. Yes, she got all the details about it. Never the couch, which everyone knew was in his office. A lot of people commented on it being there.

So, Sera had actually asked because it would come up. The younger woman had said that Harrison never sat on it and that he disliked it.

FALLING FOR THE SINGE MOM   59

Sadly, it was those words that had hurt Sera the most, not the stuff about having unprotected sex on the desk. It hurt to hear that he looked at the couch every day and disliked it because she got to look at the baby who had been conceived on that couch every day and loved her so much. Over the years, when she saw the couch, her mind would drift back to that night.

Locking her office door, she headed down the elevator to her Jeep. It had never bothered her to work late at the office; there were people around all the time, so she had never felt unsafe. Even now.

Down the street, she climbed into her Jeep and was happy she was heading home; her head was still a little dull from her birthday night. She knew she was too old to drink like that anymore.

This morning she had lied to Harrison about it being a friend's birthday because she didn't want the office to know it had been hers. Not because she had finally turned thirty-six, which felt old, but because she liked to not have the office make a fuss.

It had been Lucy and Harper who had demanded that she take the afternoon off, which she had happily done. The three of them had turned into five before school got out for the two little ones, and then even Maby had taken time from her schoolwork to head out for tacos.

So, she got to spend her birthday with all of her girls. They fought over this and that she watched them with her baby on her lap. It had been mere hours since she had seen Kylie Nash's apartment and was reminded how this day had been so close to not happening.

If she hadn't married Bradford, even if the marriage had been a fraud, she would have missed her girls. Even Emma, who was just staring at her phone and pretending not to pay attention to her older sisters, would be a different person today without them. Sera would've been different without her Lovely daughters because it was them that she had relied on every day since they came into her life. They had become her family when she had needed one the most.

Over the years, she had wondered if her parents would have gotten over what they felt was her failure if she hadn't married Bradford. The day she had told them that she was marrying Bradford Lovely, a middle-aged college professor, they had not been impressed, and she hadn't seen them since. They stopped answering calls, and she was not allowed in their house anymore. The money that was paying for her college was gone, and her bank account was suddenly empty.

From that day on, she had been on her own. They hadn't even known she was pregnant; she hadn't told them. So, when Emma was born, she didn't call them. Nor when Violet was born years later. Nor did she tell them she was a single parent to teenagers who were wild. All of it, she did on her own.

And she did a great job. Though they seemed listless, and their dedication at times to jobs was nonexistent, they were all falling into professions that they loved and excelled at, all without her pushing in one way or another. "Hands completely off" had been her motto, though, with Emma and Violet, she used a little more direction. But to her defense, they were not Lovelys.

Someday, the five older girls would move on with their lives. It didn't seem like it the next day, when all but Maby were hungover and at home all day. But today, they were all up and at it early. When she had left, Harper was already at work, and Lucy was up stuffing pork chops for a corporate event at noon. Buzz was eating breakfast with Maby and getting ready for work. Though Agatha was still sleeping, everyone knew she had been up all night working on her art, art that would take off one day in some direction no one was predicting.

On the drive home, she knew the house would be quiet when she got there. The older ones would be out on the town, except one or two who were happy to watch their baby sisters.

The wild and crazy kids she got when she got married were not what they seemed to be. They were still wild and crazy, but they were responsible and loved one another fiercely, making Sera love them all even more.

CHAPTER THIRTEEN

RAIN SPLATTERED on the window as Harrison looked at the tent in the back yard. The engagement party was supposed to be spread out and not cramped into the spacious, but not spacious enough house.

Today was the engagement party for his nephew, or was it ex-nephew now? Josh was Veronica's brother's son, but since he had been around the kid since he was young, he was considered family, which included an invite to the engagement party. An event that Harrison could have easily skipped if everyone wouldn't have assumed it was because he didn't want to see his ex. Though it would have been the reason, he didn't want her friends and family to think she had that control over him still.

So here he was at this party, which was over the top and nothing short of what he would expect from his former sister-in-law. She and Veronica were like two peas in a pod, hence the unused tent in the back yard, catered meal, and hors d'oeuvre. There was also a small band playing classical music quietly in the corner who looked just as excited as him to be there.

"At least look like you're enjoying yourself, Harrison." James slapped him on the back.

"I would be if it had been outside. More room., he admitted to his ex-brother-in-law.

"I didn't think that Veronica would be rubbing your face in the kids." James's eyes traveled to his dark-haired sister, who was dragging a blond boy of around two around and carrying a little replica in her arms. Both were in navy pants, white shirts, and little red ties. Adorable, if you were into that sort of thing.

"Didn't take her and Steven long to pop out a few, did it?" Harrison finished his drink and looked at her also, the woman he had thought he would spend the rest of his life with. From the beginning when they feared an unexpected pregnancy that years later, they would spend large amounts of money to have ... and fail at.

What he had told Sera this week had been a very condensed version of the story of his marriage. Even today, he knew that they would still be married if they had been able to have kids together. The garbage he had learned about her in the divorce would have never come out, and they would just be an old married couple now. No cheating, no huge blow-up fights over things they couldn't control. Just them still in love with one another.

But lately, the certainty of not having kids was starting to wane. The woman she had become as they divorced might have been the real woman the entire time, a woman he didn't like at all. But he had been unable to see it since she'd always been out of his reach until she looked his way one day.

It had been early fall of his sophomore year, and he had been introduced to her at a party. At the time, he had been pissed at his buddy for stealing his girl, a girl he had dated for a week. Today, he couldn't remember her name, or nearly anyone else he had slept with in college before Veronica.

But once his eyes had landed on Veronica, he was a goner. For her, he was a nobody she used to piss off her parents, which worked. Until a year later, when her father had almost died of a heart attack, and he had seen how short life was and wanted to make her his forever. Yes, they were young and had nothing, but they eloped, and her parents had to accept it.

Veronica also had to accept that he wasn't from a prominent family and never would be. It took years for her to stop trying to mold him into what she wanted in a husband. Law school had been her idea; it was a good one. Moving in with her parents had not been. He had been miserable in the big house with more space than people. Now he was able to see the house they once shared had been the same after a few years: just a place to show off their wealth, not be a family.

But they had made it through the hard times, and it had made them stronger, closer. When the harder times hit, he was unprepared for those. In the end, she had wanted something he couldn't give her, so she had left him.

Now he saw her in a different light, a dimmer light. He didn't like her, and he wondered if who he was today was just as bad as who she had been. Some days, he was sure he was.

"Nope, but you know how determined she can be. Have you met anyone yet?" James asked, his eyes moving across the room, away from Veronica and her perfect family.

Harrison had always liked Veronica's brother. He'd taken his side in the divorce, which had caused a rift in their brother-sister relationship for a time. Now they were back as close as they had been, but Harrison was still friends with James. Just not as close as they once had been.

"No, no one special." He looked around the room to avoid looking at James. The mess at work was on his mind.

His mind was playing tricks on him as they homed-in on a blonde in a jaunty ponytail carrying a tray of something around the room. She looked exactly like Sera Lovely; even her walk was the same. He followed her with his eyes as she walked and offered tiny pieces of food with a smile—Sera's smile.

"Maybe soon," James said, but Harrison couldn't take his eyes from the woman as she slipped through the kitchen door with ease. Once out of sight, he could concentrate again.

"Yeah, hopefully." Harrison had no idea what he was talking about anymore. "I have to go talk to someone."

Leaving James, one of his only friends there, he headed to the kitchen. What was the director of HR doing as a caterer? He knew she made enough money not to need a second job. Maybe she had a twin? At this point, he hoped that her twin was a little less bitchy because she was just as sexy as the original.

Glancing around the room at the other waiters, he saw a redhead with a smile. Could she be the same redhead from the night at the bar? He hadn't really been looking at her that night since her back was to him, but the hair seemed the same. There was also a black-haired woman with no smile at all.

At this point, he didn't know what he was going to say if it was her. It wasn't any of his business what she did when she wasn't working. But she had been on his mind for days, and it was more than her working on this office mess. Over the past week, he had realized that she was interesting to talk to.

"Harrison, I didn't know you were here," his ex lied as she blocked his path to the kitchen. It would have seemed casual if he didn't know her so well. Too well.

Her raven hair was in the same straight bob it had been in for years. Sleek and shiny, but severe. It accented the sharp lines of her thin face.

"I've been here the entire time." His eyes still on the kitchen door, Sera was still in there.

"I must have been too busy to notice you. I have the kids, you know. They take up so much time." She laughed as she rubbed it in his face.

"I saw that." He pulled his eyes from the kitchen door finally and looked down into her cool green eyes, the ones he once loved to stare into.

"I don't know if you know about our second, Jayden. He's three months now. And Kayden is two, almost three," the woman said.

Harrison looked from one kid to the other and wondered, *Who names their kids rhyming names?* But he knew: his ex-wife. She'd always been that way—making everything look flawless and perfect was what she thrived on.

"I didn't know, I guess. Congratulations." He pulled his eyes from the kids and looked at the kitchen door again.

"Are you here with someone, Harrison?" Of course, she knew he wasn't. She had known he was there the moment he walked in. No matter how many kids she had, she had seen him and knew what he was doing.

"Not today. My girlfriend had to work." He lied to her, and not for the first time. He didn't feel any guilt about it this time, either.

"How long have you been dating her, Harrison?" Veronica knew he was lying and wanted to trip him up. They had been married for too long and lied too much to each other for her not to.

"A few months," he said.

"Harrison, Lucy says I can be done soon. Did you want to go to your place?" Sera said with a grin, a tray still in her hand. Her perma-smile was in place, and her blue eyes were sparkling with mischief.

Trying to disguise his shock, he looked at her and mumbled, "Yes."

"Good. I hated that I had to work, but I couldn't let Lucy down today. Good help is hard to find," Sera said to his ex with a grin, which made Veronica lose hers.

"And you are?" Veronica's eyes narrowed as she looked her up and down.

"Sera Lovely. I would've thought that Harrison would have told you about me. And ... you are?" Sera asked, all innocent.

"Veronica, his ex-wife," she said between her teeth.

Over the years, he had introduced Veronica to a few of his girlfriends, and she had never had a reaction like this. This was instant jealousy, and it was new. Why would she be jealous of Sera? And why even be jealous at all? Could it be that she was nothing like the women Harrison usually dated?

"Oh, her. Harrison hasn't told me much about you at all," Seraphina said with her signature smile, dismissing Veronica as nothing special to him.

"He hasn't told me much about you either. Didn't you used to work for Rodgers and Associates also?" Veronica asked, and he looked at his ex. Did she remember this woman? It had been years since

Veronica had been to a work event with him—how was it that she remembered Sera when he barely remembered her from back then?

"Still do. I'm just helping a friend out with the catering. She can never find staff for weekends," Sera admitted, tilting the tray towards Veronica as she said it. In case his ex missed it in her hands.

"I can see that is an issue." Her voice relayed her boredom and annoyance at talking about staff issues. It was a topic she cared nothing about, never had.

"It is, but it's fun to do something different than my usual day-to-day. Gives me people-watching time," Seraphina continued, even if Veronica was getting glassy-eyed. "Well, I have to make a few more rounds, then I'll meet you in the kitchen."

With that, she actually kissed him on the cheek, brushing her breasts against his arm as she did. At that point, Harrison realized she should have been an actress because, based on Veronica's face, she bought the entire thing. More than bought it—she hated it.

"So, she finally got you." Veronica watched Sera walk around the room.

"Excuse me?"

"You're blind, Harrison. That woman wanted you years ago. Even I could see that."

"You were just jealous."

She snorted a laugh as she walked away from him, leaving him wondering what she had meant by that. For years, he didn't even know who she was, let alone have a conversation with her. And for that matter, she had been married until recently. Maybe not happily, but married.

He had only really learned who she was a few years before when she was promoted to the director job. Since then, he had thought her body was something, but her personality was above and beyond. Only recently had he seen a different side of her, a side he liked.

Since he had been invited into the kitchen, he headed that way to see what Sera said about them "dating." Pushing into the room, he was surprised at how many people were in there, but his eyes instantly found Sera, who was standing at the counter pouring champagne.

"How many need to be filled?" she called over her shoulder.

"Ten bottles, and then we can start handing them out," a blonde said from the other side of the kitchen without looking up from the sheet cake she was cutting.

"That's not a real number, Harper. Seventy-five is a real number. Ninety-four is a real number," she criticized.

"Bottles are easier to count, Sera. Just keep pouring until ten are empty, then count them and tell me how many there are. Then you'll have your real number," Harper spat back at her, making her laugh.

"The party's out there, sir." The dark-haired waitress he had seen earlier came up behind him, still not smiling.

"I was invited to the kitchen," he told her and watched as Sera set down the champagne bottle.

"By whom?" Harper demanded.

"Seraphina." He nodded at her.

"Why?" the head caterer asked, setting down her knife.

"Ask her." He grinned as she slowly turned around. Had she been caught breaking the rules? Could he be so lucky as to see that happen?

"Sera?" Harper asked.

"I might have interfered in a conversation," was all she said, the woman who had words for every situation. That was all she had as an explanation? To her boss?

"Who hasn't done that?" Harper laughed, picking up her knife again and going back to the cake. Her cuts were perfect parallel lines.

"Am I doing champagne? Where's Buzz?" The dark-haired waitress looked around, dismissing his presence. She was still not as happy as anyone else in the room.

"Yes, you are. Sera, you, and Buzz," Harper said, turning from him. He was dismissed, and even Sera went back to filling champagne.

Still standing in the middle of the room, Harrison moved over to let the women do their thing. This was way better than the party happening outside the kitchen.

A brunette came in from a side door and was slightly wet from being outside. Her arms were laden with large boxes. She didn't even glance his way as she said, "What does the groom look like?"

"Blond with brown eyes. Today he's wearing black pants and a white polo shirt," Harper said, finally done with the cake as she tossed the knife in the sink.

"I thought the shirt was blue," Sera argued, setting down an empty bottle.

"It's very light blue," The dark-haired one stated, and everyone nodded and mumbled in agreement. She must be the expert.

"I thought so. I think he currently has his tongue down Buzz's throat in the gazebo," the brunette said nonchalantly as she set down her load on the counter closest to the door.

The entire room of women hurried to the window to the back yard and peered out, all four intent on the scene. Harrison turned to look also. It wouldn't surprise him one bit; his nephew was a playboy.

What had surprised him was this wedding. From what he knew about the kid, he wasn't ready to settle down yet, and Harrison didn't want him to. Young love was fleeting. Sometimes it lasted for years, but never forever.

"Damn it!" Sera growled, grabbing a plastic bag from the counter and holding it over her head as she headed out into the rain.

He watched her rush out to the couple with her angry walk—he knew that walk well. Her hips were swaying, and he knew her breasts were heaving, even if he couldn't see them. He didn't think his nephew was old enough to face an angry Sera Lovely.

From the window, he watched her enter the gazebo and gave them a lecture they would not soon forget, based on their nods and how many times they looked at their feet. Handing off her bag to the redhead and leaving the groom to his own devices, he watched as they both came back into the house.

His nephew didn't say a thing to him or the women in the kitchen as he walked through it back to his engagement party. He quickly shot a text to James about what had just happened and watched as the sky finally opened up. Sera was in the middle of her angry walk back to the house when it hit, soaking her instantly.

Not one of the women was looking at her when she came into the house. They were all were busy getting things ready, and Buzz had taken over pouring champagne. Harrison's eyes were on her, though, or on her breasts that her wet white shirt no longer hid. Though her light blue bra did, it was giving him a perfect view of them.

"Beatrix Potter, seriously!" Sera yelled at the redhead as she pulled the wet shirt away from her skin and let it go, causing it to stick back to her skin in the exact same way it had when she had walked in the door.

"I didn't start it. I was just finishing it! He was asking for it," the woman tried to defend herself.

"Bullshit! He's practically married."

"Practically, not actually, and no way was I alone out there." The redhead smiled at Sera, making her apology a little less sincere. That just made Sera even angrier.

"Buzz can't keep it in her pants, Sera," Harper said as if it was a known fact. The brunette nodded in agreement.

"I can too! No pants were involved. It was a kiss—a bad, wet kiss. He really needs to work on those skills, or not, if he's getting married," Buzz argued with the blonde.

"Nice tits, Sera," The brunette said from in front of the tray of hors d'oeuvre.

Sera looked down at her shirt, pulled the wet material away from where it stuck to her body, and groaned, "Your just jealous, Lucy."

"Of you? Nope. Harper has the best rack of us all," Lucy said, looking over at the blonde who grinned, then grabbed hers with her hands and shook them, though there was very little movement with the chef's coat covering them.

Without looking around the room, he knew Sera's were the best in the room. Even better wet and only covered by a blue bra. They were glorious right now, and he wanted to look at them all day.

Harrison was seeing why being topless in a bar might not have embarrassed Sera at all. She and her friends were very comfortable talking about them and each other's. And maybe sex in general was a topic for everyday conversation. Either way, he liked it.

"Sera, I can't have you serve like that. This is an engagement party … that Buzz might have ended." She shot the redhead a look.

"I'm a damn good kisser, ladies. He's probably rethinking everything. If I had kissed his beloved, she would be rethinking things too. It was like his tongue was paralyzed or something." She continued to pour more booze.

"Can I leave then?" Sera asked. Though she hadn't looked at him, he knew she knew he was there.

"Yes. What you won't do to get out of work!" Harper yelled at her.

"Blame it on your baby sister, Harps." Sera pointed at the back of the redhead.

"Now I'm one short," Harper said and started taking off her perfectly clean white jacket. He was sure she would only have a bra on under the jacket, based on the group and what he knew of them. But she took it off to reveal a white button-down shirt that matched the other waiters. It seemed she was prepared to step in when needed.

"Can I go?" Sera asked again.

"Yes, go," Lucy said. She, too, was now in a waiter shirt after taking off her apron.

"She can't go! We all rode together," Buzz said, and the black-haired woman agreed.

"I can take her," Harrison interjected, knowing he would be noticed by everyone by speaking up. But he wanted away from this party, and she needed to get away from it. Win-win.

"I don't know who you are." The black-haired woman stated, looking him up and down.

"Harrison Dean. I work with Seraphina," he said, regretting saying her full name again. If they were close, he should be calling her Sera as her friends had, but the name rolled off his tongue so easily after all these years.

"If she trusts you, she can. Otherwise, you just have to stay in here until the party is over," Harper replied, filling trays with Champagne glasses.

"I don't trust him," the black-haired woman mumbled and looked him over again.

"Agatha, tray." Harper either didn't hear it or ignored it as she lifted the now-full tray towards the woman.

Sera looked at him and shrugged. "If you're willing to give me a ride, I will accept. It's across town, though."

"I live downtown, so I'm also across town." He couldn't help but be excited about spending time looking at those breasts encased in a wet bra. And he was starting to like the idea of spending time with the prude of HR, who wasn't a prude at all—just all wet.

CHAPTER FOURTEEN

THANK god Harrison's car had leather seats because she was soaking wet. Not from her initial drenching from the rain, but from the run to the car from the back door. She knew she looked like a drowned rat now.

The only consolation was that he did too. That is until he shook the rain from his hair in the car, and it had turned into completely sexy, messed-up wet hair. Hair that she wanted nothing more than to run her fingers through.

So far, during the ten-minute drive, she had been able to control her urges, though his earthy smell was intoxicating and inescapable in the small space. Added to that was the way his wet navy polo shirt clung to his body, showing her that he hadn't changed much over the years. His body was as toned as ever.

Shaking herself out of those thoughts, she reminded herself that she didn't want him in her life. Her life was great the way it was—no change needed. No need to get involved with Harrison Dean. *Especially* not with Harrison Dean.

"Do you know the bride or groom?" she asked, making conversation. She had to get her mind out of the gutter. Not that her efforts were helping; Harrison was wet!

"Groom. His dad is Veronica's brother." He grinned at her.

"Sorry about Buzz.... The kiss meant nothing to her. I know that." Even after all these years, Sera didn't know how to explain Buzz. Since she was ten years old, she'd had a hard time controlling her impulses and hadn't gotten much better since. It was what made her Buzz in the end.

"I really don't think the marriage will happen or last if it does. They've been dating for a long time, but I don't think Brad's really ready to settle down for her yet. He likes having a steady girlfriend but really likes dating also. I feel there was a bit of pressure put on by everyone around him, which won't turn out well in the end," Harrison said.

"Well, aren't you Mister Optimistic? Not all relationships end badly."

"I guess not. I just see a lot of my and Veronica's relationship in them. College sweethearts that seemed to have everything going for them … until they don't."

"Do you regret it? I mean, it ended badly, but was it always bad?" She asked because Harrison and Veronica had stayed together for years after it turned bad. What had kept them going back to each other?

"No, we had some good years. Then she wanted kids, and that was what ripped up apart." His eyes didn't leave the road as he said the words.

"Would you still be married if you had kids?"

"Probably not. There were other things that we didn't have in common after a few years. She wanted to be a society wife, and I wanted nothing to do with that." His back was stiff as he stared at the road in front of them.

"But you still do society functions," she argued. She had seen him a few times since she started helping Harper and Lucy. Usually, she tried to stay away from him if possible, not really wanting him to see her working a second job.

"Yes, but I don't like going. Especially alone."

"I've never seen you alone." She bit her lip. Had she admitted too much?

"You have catered before? At functions I've been at?" His eyes finally left the road to look her way with a smirk.

"A cater waiter only, and yes, a few over the last few months."

"I've never noticed you before."

"I've been there. Harper and Lucy started the business three years ago, and it's grown a lot in the last year. As I told your ex, help is hard to find." Even before that, when they had functions, they didn't have the money to hire extra people as waiters, so the family worked for free. Sera herself still did, though the others were paid now.

"Your friends are funny."

"I think so. I love spending time with them." You never knew how a conversation would start or end and the meanderings it would take with the girls. It had been that way when they were young, and it remained that way today.

"So, the redhead and the blonde are sisters?" he asked.

"No," she stated quickly, then corrected. "I mean, they are all sisters. All five."

"Are you one of the five sisters? I saw only four besides you," he asked.

"No, I'm not. One sister wasn't there today." She rarely told people she was their mother. Well, stepmother in reality. But with Harper being five years younger than her, it just led to complicated explanations about divorce and their actual parents. It was easier to call herself their friend, which she was happy to be.

"How long have you known them?" He stopped at a stoplight as he asked.

"Sixteen years now. They were all in high school or junior high then."

"Were you in high school then also?"

"No, Harrison, I'm the same age as you. I was in college at the time." She instantly regretted saying that. He didn't know that they were the same age.

"We aren't the same age," he argued.

"Yep. We're both thirty-six this year," she said, holding his gaze even though she knew she was blushing.

"How do you know how old I am?" he asked, taking his eyes from hers as the light turned green.

Sera looked out the windshield at the rain and tried not to say that she knew everything about him. Had for years. But all she said was, "I'm in HR, Harrison."

She had even verified that they were the same age years before when he had started at the company, and she had access to his personal file.

"Those were the women from the bar, the ones you changed shirts with?" It was as if the thought had just come to him.

"Yes, Cliff said Lucy needed a white shirt to work her shift." She rolled her eyes at the thought of Lucy's friend, though he wasn't the worst guy the girls had brought home over the years. But unlike all the others, Cliff stuck around.

"But three of you changed them," he pushed.

"Harper liked the one Lucy had on better. And Lucy's shirt was yellow, Harper's favorite color. So, we swapped shirts to the one we wanted; it just happens sometimes."

The swapping actually happened quite often. Exchanging shirts had been a constant source of fun. Everyone had their favorites, and since all the women wore basically the same size T-shirts, stealing them had become a game over the years. Every once in a while, Sera did laundry for everyone just so she could gather her favorites back. Everyone knew that was her reason for doing their laundry, but the tradeoff was worth it in their eyes.

"All the time?" he questioned.

"Most of the time, yes," she admitted, trying not to smile at all the odd locations she had sat in her bra, waiting for a shirt. "I live by the Grog, if you remember where that is."

"I might, but would it be possible to stop at my place first? It's between here and there," he asked as they hit the downtown traffic.

"I guess, but I'm soaked," she reminded him as if he hadn't been there when she had walked in the door soaking wet. At that moment, all she could feel was his eyes on her.

"I'm not likely to forget that. Your friend was right; you do have nice tits." He wasn't even looking at her when he said it.

"What?" she demanded, crossing her arms over her chest.

"Nothing," he mumbled, but she had definitely heard him and heard him correctly. It was no surprise he was looking at her chest—he had for years. It usually didn't even bother her anymore.

"No, no. You said something about my tits," she stated, even as she wished she could just let it go and not talk about it. But she was unable to keep her mouth shut. "I would appreciate it if you would not look at them all the time. It is very distracting when I'm trying to tell you something, and you're looking at my breasts and not me."

"Sorry," he mumbled, still looking at the road and not her.

"No, you aren't. What would you do if every time we had a conversation, I looked at your crotch? How would that make you feel?" she demanded. Yup, she was going there.

"Probably get an erection since I'd be looking at your tits." He looked at her breasts and smiled at his joke. She did not.

Her eyes looked at his pants to see if he had an erection; after all, he was looking at her breasts. At this point, she couldn't tell. All she could tell was that him talking about her breasts was making her nipples hard—something he could probably see though her wet shirt.

"I'm a little old for your tastes, Harrison." She folded her arms over her suddenly perky chest. "Since I can legally drink."

His laugh surprised her, then he leaned towards her and stated, eyes on her chest the entire time. "It doesn't matter your age, Sera, when your tits are that nice."

Harrison focused back on the road as he pulled into a parking garage and didn't see Sera rolling her eyes at him. "My tits don't compare to a twenty-something's. That I know."

As they drove around in circles, Sera wished she had pushed to be taken home first. Why was she always letting him get away with stuff like this? She should have just said no, that he needed to take her home.

Finally, he pulled into a spot and turned off the car. "Do you want to stay out here or come inside? I can give you a dry shirt for the rest of the ride to your place. Maybe you can give it to your friends later."

Watching him exit the car, she flung her door open. No way was she waiting for him in a creepy garage. "We don't switch just any shirt. It has to be special." And she was in no way letting go of a shirt that Harrison had owned.

Following him, she looked around the structure for flaws; things that make them fall down. Ever since she was young, she had feared underground garages. They were always collapsing in her mind, and she in no way wanted to die in one. Alone. In someone else's car.

"This way then," he said, taking her hand and leading her to the elevator bank.

With her hand encased in his, she felt the same old sensations of heat and electricity running through her body. It never failed to happen, which was why she never touched him at work. That and most of the time, if she wanted to touch him, it was to strangle him. But they weren't at work now; they were in an elevator on the way to his apartment.

The ride to the twenty-eighth floor was fast and excruciatingly slow, all at the same time. Fast because she didn't trust herself being alone with him and slow because she had to force herself not to throw herself in his arms. She hated herself for both reactions.

His hand still held hers as she leaned against the back wall of the elevator. It seemed like he was unable to let her go. The feeling was mutual. Turning to her, he ran his fingers up her damp, shirt-covered arms. He traveled across her shoulder, leaving a trail of heat and sparks as he went.

The dark blue of his eyes staring into hers with a look of desire told her that he felt it too: the pull, the draw, the need. Those same fingers brushed her neck and cheek before his lips claimed hers. Her fingers finally were able to burrow into his damp, dark hair, hair that was so familiar and so different at the same time.

His lips met hers with a hint of spice from one of the appetizers she had served, and desire erupted between them. A desire she was familiar with, because she remembered every moment of the last time they had touched like this. The intensity didn't take her by surprise this time; she was ready for it, meeting his insistent mouth with demands of her own.

Finally letting go of her, he slid his hands under her butt and lifted her to him. Sera wrapped her legs around him as he backed out of the open elevator doors into the hallway. She couldn't get close enough to him. He must have known the way blindfolded because his lips were forging a trail down her neck as he carried her to his apartment. No way was she letting go—not after all these years without him.

How he got into the apartment, or even if he shut the door, Sera would never know. She was too focused on doing all the things that had run through her mind hundreds of times over the years.

With the door closed and the keys discarded, he let her slide down his. Her feet hit the floor as her hands ran down his chest, and his hands slid under her damp blouse to cup her breasts. Moaning at the feeling, she wished her bra was gone so she could feel his hands on her body. He must have thought the same thing because he began unsnapping it as she undid the buttons up the front of her blouse.

Once the wet shirt and bra were gone, she was back in his arms as his lips suckled her nipples. She pulled at his shirt, hating the barrier between them. Even if it was only a wet piece of clothing, it was too much.

Success was hers when the shirt slipped over his head, leaving nothing between them but damp, hot skin. Skin that needed to be touched, explored. But she was too far gone for that now. She needed him.

With deft fingers, she unbuttoned and unzipped his pants, sending them to the floor with ease. The thump of his wallet on the hardwood floor went unnoticed because his hands were shedding her of her pants and panties, which got hung up on her damp legs until she bent down and pulled them off with a curse. Before she got up, she pulled a condom from her pants pocket.

Straightening, Sera turned to see Harrison standing in his boxer briefs looking her up and down. Based on the state of his obvious erection, she could tell that he liked what he saw, erasing any lingering doubt she had about her body.

Reaching up, she pulled the hair tie from her hair and tossed it on the ground, letting her damp hair tumble down her back. His eyes watched her movements as she walked toward him. The feeling of power and making him want her was overwhelming. Her, Sera Lovely.

Grinning, she asked, "Do you think you can handle this, Harrison?"

His eyes swept her body again. "I think I can, Sera."

Dragging his boxers down his legs, she whispered as she slid the condom on him, "I'll wreck you for everyone else."

Grabbing her under her arms, he pulled her to him so that her core was cradling his cock. So close, and yet still so far away. Sera wrapped her legs around him as she sought his mouth, kissing him deep and hard as she rubbed her wet core against his erection. The movement was enough to make her moan into his mouth.

With her still wrapped around him, he moved farther into the apartment, but he only made it two steps before he stopped. She had shifted and rubbed until his shaft had slid home, and he was nestled deep inside her.

"Sera," he groaned as she worked her body against his to slide him in and out.

Grabbing her ass, he stopped her. "Stop, or I'll cum, and I want this to last," he growled in her ear, making her grin. That was exactly how she wanted him.

"Cum for me, Harrison. We have all day." She scraped her teeth against his shoulder as she constricted the walls of her core, making him shudder and groan.

At her words, he pounded into her, using her hips as leverage. When his fingers slipped across her clit, it was her turn to gasp. Within moments, she was panting his name as she came. Instantly, he too was cumming as she clung to him.

As she tried to regain her breath, he walked them through his beautiful apartment into his bedroom. Harrison fell backwards onto the bed with her still deep inside her body.

"Holy fuck, woman," he breathed.

"I warned you." She laughed as she planted kisses on his chest and shoulders, not ready to be done with him. Hell, she had barely started. There were a lot of years of fantasies to live out today.

"I should've known you would be truthful." His hands ran up her sides and cupped her breasts, running his thumbs over her nipples.

Sera had to close her eyes against the sensation of his hands on her body. It was even better than her dreams had been. Even the memories of the last time paled in comparison—so much better, and she never wanted it to stop. But for today, it didn't have to.

CHAPTER FIFTEEN

HARRISON'S EYES flew open when he realized he was alone in bed. The coldness crept into his heart as he listened for sounds of her moving in the apartment. Not that they had talked about the morning over the course of the previous afternoon and evening, but she didn't have a car at his place.

A smile curved his lips as he let his mind drift back to the day before. She had been so right about him dating the wrong women— they were nothing compared to Sera Lovely.

Sera had him tied down and naked when she demanded that he never, ever call her Seraphina again. At that point, he would have happily agreed to anything she asked of him, and not because he was tied up and helpless, but because she asked with her constant smile and bright blue eyes. Then she had taken him in her mouth, making him fight against his restraints so he could touch her.

Groaning at the images that flashed through his mind when he was finally free, he wondered again where she could be. He needed her desperately. Again.

His eyes were adjusting to the darkness when she walked naked into the room with her phone to her ear, half her face glowing from the light. If she was talking, it was too quiet to hear because he heard nothing before she pulled the phone from her ear and sat on the bed.

"I have to go. Agatha is picking me up." She shut the phone off, sending the room into total darkness again, and tossed it on the bed as she spoke.

"I can take you home, Sera." He ran his fingers down her smooth, bare back.

"No need. Agatha just got off work and will swing by and pick me up."

"Was Agatha at the party yesterday?" he asked, realizing a lot had happened since he had first seen her the day before at the party. He didn't even know if the wedding was canceled because of the kiss.

"Yep. Black hair, no smile." What she had left out was that Agatha was also judgmental and seemed to already hate Harrison.

"Let me take you home later." He pulled her back onto the bed, making her laugh.

"Not today, Harrison." Her hand cupped his cheek, and then she climbed out of bed. "I have things I need to get done before work starts again."

"That should be fun." He stated, watching her put on her panties and black slacks again. For a few minutes longer, he got to enjoy her breasts while she searched for her bra. After giving up, she just pulled on the white shirt she had been wearing at the party the day before and started to button it up. From across the room, it looked dry. Wrinkled, but dry.

"It'll be okay. I should have done them yesterday. Laundry is going to take all day now, but Harper needed help." She shrugged.

"And then I didn't let you leave the rest of the day."

"Yes, I spent the rest of the day with you," she admitted.

"Can I call you?" He climbed out of bed and took her in his arms.

Just being able to touch her felt right, like she was the thing that had been missing in his life until today. It was as if he'd started seeing the world as a different place when she was near him, touching him. He couldn't believe he had missed this feeling in all the years he had known her.

"I don't know why you would want to, Harrison. This was a one-time thing, right?" She pulled out of his arms and looked at her phone for a moment. Her words were nothing but dismissing.

"One time?" He looked at her in disbelief. He didn't want to stop until he'd had his fill and was starting to think that that would never happen. Right now, he couldn't even remember how many times they had sex the night before, but each time had been better than the last.

"We just let our hormones get the best of us. We can't have a relationship."

"Why not?"

"We work together, and I'm overseeing your harassment claim and all it entails." She took a step away from him.

Was she actually talking about this while he was naked? Like anything that had happened between them in the last twenty-four hours had anything to do with work or that claim.

"Agatha's here. I had a good time." Her phone buzzed in her hand as she talked as if they had just met. That it had been a hookup, a fling. Nothing more than a few hours of fun.

"Yeah, see you around."

Harrison was hurt and stayed in the bedroom, unable to watch her walk away from him. This was not how he expected the morning to go. He had expected her to stay in his bed all day today also. Instead, she had dismissed him from her life.

Hearing the door shut as she left his apartment, he fumed at the woman. Had she not felt what he had felt touching her the day before? Was he alone in his reaction to her? Did she not feel the pull to be together? The moment he had taken her hand, everything had changed. Yes, he had been attracted to her before that, but when he touched her, the attraction bloomed, exploded.

Looking back on it, he didn't even know how they had gotten into the apartment. All he had seen was her. All he wanted to see was her.

And she'd felt nothing?

CHAPTER SIXTEEN

"Did he make you cry, Mom?" Agatha said as Sera slid into the passenger seat of the blue Jeep. It was Maby's vehicle, but the sisters just took whatever vehicle they wanted to use all the time. Cars were just a way to get places.

"No." She looked out the passenger window at Harrison's building as Agatha drove away, not letting Agatha see her wipe her eyes.

Yes, it had been as intense and memorable as the last time, but this time, she was in a different place in life. Last time, he hadn't really known who she was. This time, they were sober, and she had her job. And part of her job right now was investigating him.

Agatha shook her head at her mom. Over the last few months, Agatha had settled down more and had actually put on weight, making her look healthier than she had in years. She'd always known more about Sera than the other kids did, including that Harrison was the father of the little girls.

"Not as good as you remembered?" Agatha asked as she drove through the dark streets.

"It was better," Sera admitted. "But it was only a one-day thing."

"For you or for him? He seemed pretty into you yesterday."

Agatha's eyes were on the road, not looking over at Sera as she wiped her tears on her sleeve.

"We work together, Ag," was all Sera said.

"Work together well? Or is he an ass at work?" Agatha asked.

"He can be an ass, but there's more to it than that," Sera admitted.

"Are you pregnant?" Agatha cracked a smile at her question.

"I hope not." Sera sighed, happy she had insisted he wear a condom every time. Even if she was on the pill, she wasn't taking chances. Birthing three of his babies would make it look like an addiction.

"I'm just going to say you are until you can prove to me you are not," Agatha said as she pulled in front of the house, reminding Sera of the fact that every other time she had slept this this man, she had gotten pregnant, something that only Agatha knew beyond Sera herself.

"You cannot stop me from drinking, Ag," Sera said as she threw open her door.

"I will too stop you," Agatha said as she followed her into the house.

"No need, Ag. I'm not!" she called over her shoulder as she opened the door. It was always open since there was always someone at home. None of the girls had regular hours or the same schedule. Someone was almost always here, and if not, there was nothing to steal anyway.

Once the door was open, Sera heard voices in the kitchen. Even though it was 5:30 in the morning, there were already people up. Going straight in to see who was up, she saw that Harper and Lucy were already working, peeling vegetables and chopping them up.

"Morning, girls," she said as she slid onto a stool.

"Morning. Didn't think you'd be home this early," Lucy said from the sink. No judgement, just a statement.

"I wanted to spend the day with my girls. I missed all day yesterday and Friday. I worked late," she said because they might not have even realized she had been gone. They had their own lives, after all.

"How was yesterday? He was very good looking." Harper pointed the knife she was holding at her.

"Good, it was a nice day. Is the wedding still on?" she dodged.

"Nope, it was Buzzed!" Lucy made a buzzing sound over the potato she was peeling.

"Buzz." Sera shook her head at Buzz. She wasn't exactly known for thinking before doing. It usually got her in over her head quickly.

"We got her home and away from him, but he's constantly calling now. She must be one great kisser," Harper said sarcastically.

"It's the red hair. Guys think she'll be freaky in bed." Lucy shrugged at the idea.

"I don't know why men don't realize it's the blondes in this family that are freaky in bed. Right, Sera?" Harper grinned at her fellow blonde.

"Mom's freaky between the sheets?" Cliff Scott said from the doorway.

It didn't surprise Sera that the man had spent the night in the house. What surprised her was that he *continued* to sleep at the house. Lucy had a boyfriend, and it wasn't Cliff. Both always denied that anything was happening beyond Cliff crashing after a late night at work or after they had been out partying.

"I'm going to start charging you rent, Cliff," Sera said to him like she always did.

"I'll pay you to show me your kinky moves, Mom Lovely." He winked at her.

"You'll just have to live with listening to them through the walls, Cliff," Sera said. She knew the walls were thin, and Lucy's bedroom was on the other side of hers.

"Lucy said you nabbed a man at the party yesterday. Good job." Cliff held up his hand for a high five that Sera didn't return.

"I don't want to talk about it," Sera replied, and all the woman in the room looked at her in confusion. She was usually willing to share details, even just a few.

"Someone special, then?" Harper was the first to ask. She was always the pushiest.

"I just don't want to talk about it yet. It only happened yesterday." She was sure she would never want to share details about her time with Harrison with her daughters. It was too special for that.

"Are you going to see him again?" Lucy's eyes sought out her sisters as she dared ask.

"No, it was just a one-night thing."

"One day and a night thing; you could have stayed. We're here for the girls all day. Or someone should be. We have an event tonight."

"I want to spend the day with them. I promised a movie day today before I left yesterday. Disney princesses and teen love all day for me," Sera assured them as she stood up from her stool.

"With that, I'm out," Cliff said with a wave to everyone, not even a backwards glance for the woman who shared her bed with him overnight, or at least part of the night. Who knew when Lucy actually got up to start prepping.

Sera watched him go and asked not for the first time, "What is up with you and Cliff?"

Lucy finally looked up from her chopping and looked around the room at everyone looking at her. "He's my best friend, and his room-mate has no respect for communal spaces and has his chick over all the time. Even I've seen them naked, and I'm barely over there."

"Mom wants to know if you two are fucking," Harper said as she waved a spatula at Lucy.

Since day one, Harper had an in-your-face, take-no-prisoners atti-tude. Being the oldest of the group of wild kids, she often took charge —and still did, if you asked her.

"No, we're not. I don't think of him like that. We are just friends." Lucy gave a little shake at the image in her head, which was the same reaction Sera would have about sleeping with the man. It just wasn't going to happen. But then again, Lucy hung out with him nearly every day or night, usually.

"But he sleeps with you?" Sera asked.

"Sleeps. Not anything else." Lucy didn't seem to notice that it was weird.

"Okay," Sera said, letting it go for another day. Lucy had no reason to lie to her; sex was allowed in the house. He seemed to be an okay guy but also didn't seem all that into Lucy either—that was what worried Sera the most. Lucy deserved someone who was completely into her, though Lucy's track record wasn't great. All the men she dated treated her like garbage, and she took it.

Heading upstairs for a shower, she tiptoed past Buzz, who was sleeping in Sera's bed. Since the house was one room short, she typically slept on the couch, but if someone was going to be out all night, Buzz took their bed. Apparently, that meant Sera's last night.

It had been two years since Buzz's last relationship had fizzled, and she had moved back in. But every time she started planning on moving the little girls together, one of the older girls would meet someone. There would be talk of moving out for a while, but then nothing. The relationship was over.

Not that Buzz ever complained about bed-hopping, which actually was a lie. She complained all the time, but not enough to move out, which meant she was okay with it, right?

After her shower, the redhead was up and gone, giving Sera her room back to herself, leaving her alone as she tried not to let ending whatever happened with Harrison yesterday upset her. It was better to be done with him now before it lasted a few weeks, and he dumped her like he did with everyone else since his divorce. She didn't want to be the next on that list.

Downstairs, all the girls were up and eating breakfast as Harper and Lucy continued to work. Emma was eating cereal and ignored her mom, who gave her an unreturned hug. Violet, on the other hand, was all in on the hug and chatted to her mom about what she had done the day before. Neither mentioned that *she* hadn't been there the day before.

Once breakfast was over, she settled in with the girls for a movie day. With Violet right beside her, they started the first princess movie on the list as Emma rolled her eyes. But soon they were all into the action, and Buzz and Agatha joined them.

Kissing the top of Violet's hair that was so much like her father's,

Sera felt the need to tell him about the children he fathered. He was missing everything they did, and every day, he missed a little more. It wasn't even the big things; it was just Emma telling the princess not to trust the bad guy or Violet's little body pressed to hers. He was missing it all.

CHAPTER SEVENTEEN

ON SUNDAY after she had left, he had fumed for hours about her abrupt departure, questioning why she had left. His mind could only say it was because she either had something going on like she had said, or she felt it was a big mistake. Whatever the reason, all he wanted to do was talk to her about it.

To him, it hadn't been a big mistake, and he couldn't stop thinking about it. It wasn't even the sex; it was everything about her. Her feistiest, her enthusiasm, her uninhibited personality … everything wrapped in one person.

After a few hours of stewing over what little he knew about the woman, he decided to put her out of his mind and go for a drive, but his car still seemed damp and smelled of her perfume as he drove a few miles trying not to picture her there with him, wet.

His mind drifted to the moments before she had walked out on him. In that moment, he had never wanted her to leave. That had scared him. Not once since his marriage had fallen apart had he wanted to spend more time with a woman he was seeing. Usually, he preferred them to leave his bed without any fuss. At least until it was Sera walking out his door before sunrise with no plans to ever return again.

Suddenly all he wanted to do was spend all his time with her—make breakfast for her and linger over coffee as they talked about everything, or spend the day doing what she wanted to do and hoping to end the day together. Instead, she was gone.

Harrison pulled into the short driveway of a little yellow Cape Cod with blue trim, completely out of place in Minnesota. As he climbed out of his car, he could hear someone in the neighborhood mowing their lawn, and Harrison could smell the crisp scent of freshly cut grass in the air.

Before he could even knock on the door, it opened to reveal a smiling face that always put a grin back on his. Emily Dean had no idea he was coming to visit today, yet his unexpected visit hadn't seemed to surprise her.

"Harry! You didn't call." She stepped back from the door and let him inside.

"I guess I should have. You could've had company," he teased her. After thirty years as a single mom, as far as he knew, she hadn't started dating again.

"No company but you, and you're my favorite company," his mom gushed and gave him a hug.

Her arms around him was enough to make him feel better for a moment. "Thanks, Mom. You do know how to make a man feel loved."

"You are loved, Harry. I love you every day. Even when you don't call or stop by very often," she scolded him mildly.

"I'm sorry, Mom." He knew he should call her more often, but life sometimes got in the way.

"Come and sit in the kitchen. I was making cookies. We can talk." She walked away from him, and he followed like he always had.

When he had been thirteen, he had grown taller than his mom, but she still was able to control him with just a few words. Her dark hair matched his until gray had overtaken hers after he was an adult. In his mind, he still saw her as the woman she had been when he had still lived in the small apartment with her, miles and a lifetime from where they were now.

Once in the kitchen, he saw she was in the middle of not just one batch of cookies but two or three different kinds. The room was warm from the oven, but the entire scene took him back to his childhood, watching or helping her bake. She had always loved to bake. Her day job could have been anything, but baking was one of her passions. One of the many passions she had to forgo to make a barely livable wage for years.

"So, what brings you over today? You don't just stop by much. Getting married?" Her gray eyes lit up at the thought. She had never married but was always ready for him to be married again.

"Nope, nothing that bad. Not even seeing anyone, really," he said, watching her scoop out even-sized balls of batter to put on a cookie sheet.

"Really? What does that mean? You either are or not," Emily stated.

"It's complicated."

"Everything is."

"Why didn't you ever date after Dad left?" he asked. He had never questioned anything about the man who had walked out on his mom when he was four. He just knew it had happened, and that Emily Dean was the best mom ever. He had never missed having a dad around. Mom was there.

Her eyes went to the bowl in front of her, and she didn't look back at him. "It's complicated."

"Everything is." He shot back at her, making her chuckle.

"I guess you are all grown up now," she said to her thirty-six-year-old son. "Your father was not a nice person, Harry. I left him more than once, and he would get me to come back, mostly for you. 'A boy needs a father,' he would always tell me, but you didn't need him as a father. He was very abusive in every way. I will not go into it, but after I finally broke it off in the end, I never found someone I could trust again. It's as simple as that."

"You never even hinted anything about that." Harrison was shocked by her words. He had just assumed the man had walked away and never looked back, not that his mom had ran from him as fast as she could.

"I didn't want you to think poorly of him. He *was* your father."

"I don't even think about him ever," Harrison admitted. He had one parent, always had.

"I do." His mom actually smiled at her admission. "You turned out exactly like I had always wanted him to be. I am proud of you."

"Don't be. I'm under investigation at work for sexual harassment," he admitted. He didn't want her to know, but if he couldn't prove the claim was false, then he would have to tell her.

"Did you?" was all she said. No judgment in her eyes.

"No. A woman accused me of having an affair with her and getting her pregnant."

"Did you?"

"No, I never touched her, and you know I can't have kids."

"No, I know you have a *small chance* of having kids. I haven't given up on you like Veronica did. I believe in you."

"In me getting someone knocked up?"

"Of you giving me some grandkids."

"I wouldn't hold your breath."

"I am anyway. So, who is it you're seeing, or not?"

"Just a woman I've known for years, but suddenly she is different."

"Different good or different bad?"

"Bad, in a good way." He laughed at his mom's expression. "She works in HR and is actually handling the harassment case."

"That doesn't sound good, but tell me about her anyway," his mother said.

"Let's see. Her name is Sera, and she's blonde and tall. For some reason, she's always smiling—actually, she's usually laughing when she's not at work. She's the head of HR, but yesterday, she was waitressing for a friend who needed help. She was so different out of the office. We're the same age, so a little different than the type of women I've been dating lately," he answered, remembering her wet in James's kitchen.

"Sounds like someone you could have a future with. And nothing like Veronica," his mom said, not trying to hide that she didn't like his ex-wife. Her dislike of the woman had been a surprise to him after all her years of pretending otherwise. Apparently, she was a good actress.

"She isn't. Most likely raised with little to no money, and she seems so down to earth and normal. Nothing like Veronica and her friends."

"I might like her. Maybe you can pursue her after your harassment thing is over."

"Nope, she just told me it was a one-night thing."

"Probably because of the case. She doesn't want to seem like she's on your side. She has to be fair since that's her job."

"Maybe, I don't know."

"I do. She sounds smart and doesn't want her personal life to interfere with her work life. Just let her be until this all blows over, then get her. I want to meet her," she said with a grin. "Does she have any kids?"

"I don't know. She's never mentioned any, but I think so. I remember her being pregnant once years ago." He should have asked. He never even thought about it until this moment. They had been busy doing and talking about other things.

"I hope so. I want grandkids from you."

"Maybe after all this blows over, I will ask," he said, realizing his mom was right, as usual. He needed to stay away from her until this was over, and then he would get her back in his bed. Where she belonged.

"If that's all, I think you can mow the lawn so I can work on these cookies. When you get done, I will make your favorite ones, so you can take them home with you." His mom winked at him. She may not have been expecting him, but she had a list of things for him to do anyway.

"I will do that, just for you." Harrison did everything his mother asked the rest of the afternoon, but not one task managed to take his mind off Sera Lovely.

Now that he was back in the office on Monday, he really was trying to follow his mother's advice. He was. He wasn't going to talk to Sera about the case or them; he just wanted to talk to her for a moment. But the closed door meant it wasn't happening.

Once in his office, he tried to concentrate on his work. Maybe she would come seek him out. She knew where he was just as he knew where she was. And his door was open!

CHAPTER EIGHTEEN

MONDAY DRAGGED on for Sera since the progress reports were finally complete. That left her to concentrate on the harassment claim, which was the one thing that she didn't want to think about anymore.

Since Sunday morning, she had thought about nothing but Harrison and sex, but not the way she should've been thinking about it. She should be concentrating on the accusations that he'd been having sex with his barely legal personal assistant.

So far today she hadn't seen him, though she had thought she would've the moment she got there. After she had left him so angry on Sunday morning, she was sure he would be out for blood this morning, but she hadn't heard a peep from him.

She was waiting on the paternity test, and then next week, she was going to talk to Harrison again to make sure his answers were the same, leaving her to do her usual work for the first time in a week. But she was unable to get back in the swing of things all day.

The clock struck 5 p.m., and Sera grabbed her briefcase but knew she would not be working once she got home. She was just taking it home to look good if she ran into a partner on the way out of the building.

That should make her feel bad, but she had things to do at home.

Not many, but enough that it would keep her busy. Her mind was on the task in front of her and not the group waiting for the elevator when the hairs on the back of her neck stood up.

Turning slowly, she saw Harrison standing just behind her. After the weekend, her body was on sharp alert for him. Though he was practically standing close enough to touch her, he didn't say anything as the elevator doors swished open and the crowd got in, squeezing close to everyone.

In the tight space, they stood face-to-face, their bodies pressed close to each other. His smell invaded her, and her mind went back to being in his bed, his body pressed to hers. His blue eyes on hers, just like right now.

By the time they made it to the lobby, her breath was short, and her body was humming with need for him. A need she couldn't do anything about. It had been her that had ended it and with good reason, but right now, her body was arguing with her. His body pulled away from hers, leaving behind cold in its wake.

With shaky legs, she headed for the door with the crowd from the elevator. Her car was parked a block away, and she needed the walk to get her hormones under control, which was hard—very hard.

Once at her Jeep, she opened the door. No need to lock a twenty-year-old Jeep with nothing in it; nobody was taking anything from it or stealing it. Tossing her briefcase in the back, she slammed the door shut and ran right into the man whose body hers craved.

Harrison's arms went around her. Whether it was to stop her from falling or just to pull her to him, she didn't know, but the action did both. Her body instantly responded, and her hands grabbed his hips, unable to not touch him.

"I came to talk to you in private." His voice was husky and deep. Despite the words he spoke her body was on fire from them.

His words alone should have stopped her movement, but her mind wasn't in control anymore. So, she pressed her body to his, needing to connected to him again. It had been ages. It had been well over a day, nearly two.

"We can't," she whispered. Whether she meant touch or talk, even she couldn't say. Both were true, but neither seemed to matter.

"I know," he admitted, just holding her close. "Come to my place."

"No, we can't. Once was a mistake, twice ..." She trailed off. His lips had touched her forehead, and her thoughts froze at the contact.

"I know, but—" He stopped, unable to say what they both knew.

"I will come or chicken out," she admitted. She knew what she should do, but it wasn't what she wanted to do.

With her words, he pushed her away and walked away without a word. Unable to watch him, she climbed into her Jeep and headed out of the parking lot, her mind in turmoil. She blindly followed him as he drove to his apartment building and found a parking spot close to it.

Sera gave herself a short lecture during the equally short walk into the building about how wrong this was and how if they were found out, it could be bad for both of them. But her feet kept moving.

The sight of him waiting for her when she walked into the lobby made her forget every argument. His eyes were on her as she rushed toward him, giving in to the pull that was always there. She was now sure he felt it also.

"You came?" he questioned, though it wasn't a question he needed to ask.

"Yes," she answered as he took her hand and led her to the elevators.

With half a dozen people in the elevator this time, she was just happy to hold his hand. They weren't the only ones to get out of the elevator on his floor, and he continued to hold her hand as they walked to his apartment. Once the door was closed behind them, all pretense that they could do anything but let their bodies have their way flew out the window.

It wasn't until after seven that she had found time to text the girls that she wouldn't be home that night. She had barely sent before Harrison pulled her away again, and she wasn't able to get to her phone for another few hours.

CHAPTER NINETEEN

AFTER A WEEK of Sera spending every moment not at work with Harrison, she put her foot down and said she needed to go home for more than five minutes. Since it was Saturday, and they were actually able to spend the entire day together without having to bother with work, her words pissed Harrison off. Just as they had on the previous Sunday.

It was becoming obvious that he was jealous of her time away. He had no idea where she went or who she spent time with. On Wednesday, she had gone back to her place for a few hours, and he found himself pacing until she returned. Not that he didn't trust her, but he had never missed anyone like he missed her.

For an instant, he had thought about tying her to his bed for the day and not letting her go, but he was sure that would just piss her off. Though after a week, he also knew it would turn her on just as much.

Now Sera had been gone a few hours, and he was antsy. She had said she would come back on Sunday afternoon and spend the night with him, but Sunday was an entire day away.

After folding the laundry that he had forced himself to do, he put it away and began pacing again, wondering if she felt the same way he did. What he did know was that after this stupid harassment thing was over, he was having her move in with him, or he was moving in with her. After a week, he was already done with the entire "your place and my place" thing.

Since his divorce, he hadn't met anyone he had wanted to spend more than a few hours at a time with. Even his ex sometimes got on his nerves, and he had to take a walk to get away. But Sera was completely different. He craved being with her.

Deciding he could get more done at the office than here, and probably pace less, he headed out of the quite, lonely apartment, a quality he once loved about the place. Rarely had he gone to the office on a Saturday, and never had he went in jeans and a T-shirt, but he wasn't changing. Nobody should be there anyway on a Saturday afternoon.

Harrison pulled into the parking lot that Sera always parked in. He now used it, even if they had stopped walking together to their cars after the first day. Usually, she let him get a half an hour head start before she came to his place. Then in the morning, she rushed home for about an hour before coming to work. But just parking in the same area made their relationship seem more real, even if it wasn't when they were together at work.

He knew she wouldn't be at the office, but he checked for her Jeep anyway. No red ones today, but there was a silver one that looked similar in the lot. Smiling at the coincidence, he walked to the building. Her driving the beat-up old car was still odd, even if she had explained that her dad loved them and that she had learned as a teenager how to fix them when something went wrong. So far, he hadn't seen her do it, but was sure she was telling the truth.

Once in the elevator, his mood lifted a little. It would be nice to lose himself in work for a while before giving her a call this evening to see if she was willing to come back early. Maybe by then, her chores would be done.

His tennis shoes made no noise as he headed toward his office. The place was eerily silent, and he wondered if the office was haunted because it felt occupied even when empty of people. This was why he didn't usually come in on a Saturday.

His office door was open, but he knew he had shut it. The cleaners must have left it open in error. It didn't matter; his filing cabinet was locked, and there was nothing confidential sitting out. It was just an annoyance.

Looking out his window with a smile, he knew Sera was out there somewhere. He needed to get her address so that he actually knew where that was. After a week, he still knew very little about her. Talking had not been a priority most days.

Sitting down in his chair, movement dragged his eyes to his couch. A dark-haired teenager dressed mostly in black was looking at him over a book she was reading. Her blue eyes showed some surprise.

"Who are you?" he asked, jumping from his chair as she scrambled off the couch and dropping the book.

"Holy fuck!" the kid yelped as she headed for the door, but he was closer to it and managed to snag the sleeve of her skinny black T-shirt as she tried to rush past him.

"*Who are you?*" he asked again.

Now what? He had caught her, but to what end? He had no place to take her.

"Let go of me, perv!" Yelling at him as she tried to wiggle free, she was stronger than he would have assumed she would be. She was almost pulling free.

"You were in *my* office, kid!" he snarled and tightened his grip. Security could deal with her; that's what they were there for. "*Who are you?*"

She clawed at him until he had to grab hold of her other arm, and then she started kicking him with her oversized boots. He started to drag her down the hallway toward the elevator and the security desk in the lobby. She was fighting him with every step.

"Let her go, Harrison!" Sera yelled at him from down the hallway. There was an anger in her voice he knew well.

At the sound, he let go of the kid, and she scrambled away from him as fast as her legs could take her, rushing toward Sera's voice. Turning around, he saw Sera in blue jeans and a bright green shirt, the teenager behind her, and a smaller version of the teen in her arms.

"Mom, he's a fucking perv! I don't know where he was taking me," the teen said to Sera.

"I was taking her to security. She shouldn't be in my office," he explained the misunderstanding.

"Then don't have a couch in your office, perv!" the kid shot back at him from behind the protection of Sera.

"Stop it!" Sera said and put the littler girl down on the floor. "Emma, get your book and take Violet to my office. I need to talk to Harrison."

He watched as the teen mumbled something and took the littler bouncing girl by the arm and slipped into his office, then quickly exited with a book in her hand. He watched them walk to Sera's office. The little one looked back frequently.

"Sorry about Emma. She was just reading and not messing with anything. I can assure you she has no interest in anything in your office. I was just catching up on some work, and then we were going out for coffee," Sera explained with her arms folded over her chest, covering the saying on her yellow T-shirt.

"She just surprised me. I wasn't expecting anyone to be here," he admitted.

"I should've worked late on Friday, but I didn't." No need to say where she had been that night—he knew.

"Did she call you mom?" he asked the one question that he wanted to know the answer to. Neither child looked much like her, but if the teenager was, then the other had to be as well because they looked alike. And both had looked to Sera for protection.

"Yes, Emma and Violet are my children," was all she said. They had been inseparable for nearly a week, and she had never mentioned kids. He'd known she had at least one. Two was a surprise.

"You never said."

"I don't like to introduce them early in a relationship. I didn't know if you would understand." She shrugged.

"I would like to get to know them, but not until you're ready," he replied, knowing people were often cautious when it came to their kids. "Are there any more?"

Kids with Sera had been a possibility, but one that he had put out of his head every time he thought of it. Now he had to start thinking of her as a mother with kids who already needed her, kids that he had to decide if he wanted to be a part of their lives. Because if he wanted Sera, he had to take on them, no questions asked.

"No, just the two." Her eyes darted to her office where a little face was peeking out at them.

"Can I meet them, or is it too soon? It's up to you, Sera." He wanted to know everything about the woman in front of him, and that included her kids. But he didn't want to push her or scare her at all. He saw her for what she was: an overprotective mom. And he loved her for it.

Her eyes closed for a moment before she said, "If you want."

"I do. It would have been fine if you would've told me," he said.

"You don't really date women who have kids." She shrugged and headed for her office.

"Maybe they just never told me about them," he shot back at her.

"Very funny, Harrison."

The little one darted out of Sera's office and ran into her arms. She easily lifted her onto her hip. Deep blue eyes peered at him from over her mom's shoulder.

Without trying to stare, he tried to find any features of Sera in the little girl. Possibly the nose was all he came up with. They both must look exactly like their father, whoever he was.

In her office, the teen was sitting behind her mom's desk, her nose back in the book. Looking up as they entered, he was still surprised that this was Sera's daughter. Though he wasn't a good judge for the ages of kids, this girl was probably almost driving.

"Harrison, this is Emma, and Violet is almost eight." Sera gestured to the kids, not saying the age of the older one. On purpose, or not?

"Sorry I tried to take you to security, Emma," he said, trying to get on her good side. He knew teens were harder to win over.

"Emma wasn't supposed to be in there anyway," little Violet said from her mom's arms.

"Shut up, Violet," Emma snapped at her baby sister.

"I can talk as much as I want. I can talk forever if I want to. You aren't the boss of me," Violet replied to her sister, which just made the older girl madder.

"Hush, Violet," Sera said and put her down again. This time, the little girl left her side and hopped on the guest chair in front of the desk, her pink shoes swinging in the air.

"Harrison wants to go have coffee with us," Sera said.

"The perv?" Emma's eyes looked him over, and based on her expression, had found him lacking.

"He's not a pervert, Emmaline. Maybe if you were nice to him, he would let you go into his office when I bring you. No sneaking involved," Sera pointed out.

"Is it really worth it if you aren't sneaking around?" Emma replied to her mom, trying to get a rise from the woman, who didn't take the bait.

"I'm okay with going with the perv, but I'm still not getting coffee," Violet said, foot still swinging.

"Girls, his name is Harrison, and stop calling him a perv. Violet, you can have hot coco like always," Sera said.

"If I can have a large coffee, I'm in," Emma said, finally closing her book.

"I'm buying, so you can have anything you want," Harrison answered, trying to please her.

"Cake?" Violet asked with excitement.

"He said *anything*," Sera replied in a tone that sounded like he would regret the offer.

Emma got up and said, "I'm sitting at my own table. I don't eat with pervs."

Sera's only reaction was to shoot her daughter a look and shake her head. The girl shot the same look back at her mom, and they just stared at each other. A standoff.

"Me too." Violet jumped down from her chair. She rushed ahead of them with her black curls bouncing to hit the button for the elevator, then bounced as she waited for them to come. Emma, on the other hand, ignored the adults and put headphones in her ears as she followed them.

The elevator was quick since the building was mostly empty, and soon, they were heading toward a coffee shop a few blocks down that Harrison didn't even know about.

Sera walked beside him but had remained silent as they went, letting Violet dominate the conversation, which the kid was an expert at. She had a lot to say about almost everything, and as she spoke, her little feet were constantly moving.

Then she ran ahead to the end of the block, only to turn back around and run back. "How do you even keep up with her?"

"Emma was the same way until twelve, then it wears off and turns snarly." She shot her oldest a grin, but the kid ignored her mom or didn't hear.

Harrison took Sera's hand in his, and he was happy she didn't pull away. She just letting their steps match as they strolled. "Five more years?"

"It goes quickly," was all she said, watching the girl run.

"So, how old were you when you had Emma?" He chanced a look back at the teen still walking behind them.

"Almost twenty." Sera also looked back with a smile.

"Married at nineteen and a baby right away?"

"I was already pregnant when I got married," she admitted, but knowing how young she was, it didn't surprise him.

"Have you ever introduced them to anyone?" He wanted to know if she kept them from everyone or just him because he worked with her. She never brought her personal life with her to work if she could help it.

"Both of them? No. I did introduce Emma to a man before I had Violet," she said, letting Violet push the button for the crosswalk.

"Weren't you still married?" He knew she was. Her divorce was six years before, and this kid was almost eight.

"It was an unusual marriage.... I don't want to go into it right now." She dropped his hand to grab a hold of Violet's as they walked across the street. Once across, she let her daughter's go and took his again.

With her evasive words, he wanted to push. What had made the marriage unusual? Had she gone through a long divorce just like his, and they accidentally had a kid in the middle of it? So many questions, but with her kids near, there would be no answers.

Emma finally picked up her pace as the coffee shop drew near, bumping his shoulder as she passed them, and not by accident. He let her; she was just protecting her mom the only way she knew how. And for some reason, he liked her doing it.

In line, the girls chatted with their mom about what they could order. Sera once again picked up Violet and pointed at stuff on the menu. The girl seemed too large to be held like Sera was, but Harrison didn't know much about kids, so he didn't say anything. But when Sera put her down, Violet asked Harrison to pick her up. With an odd flutter, he picked her up, and it felt like they had done this a hundred times. Like she was his kid.

With orders placed and tables chosen, Emma's across the walkway from theirs, Violet snuggled back into her mom's arms, just looking at him.

"What grade are you in, Violet?" he asked.

"No grade," she said with the most serious face.

"Don't be stupid. It's summer. She will be in second this fall," Emma answered, even if her headphones were in.

"I am not stupid, Emma. I am smart—my teacher says so," the little girl argued. It seemed they argued a lot, and it didn't bother their mom in the least.

"All teachers say that, Violet." Emma opened her book and buried her nose back in it.

"Not to everyone. Violet is smart, Emma, as are you," Sera said, trying to stop them.

"How about you, Emma? What grade are you in?" Harrison turned to her, and her blue eyes looked up from the pages of her book.

"Tenth, this fall. And you don't have to be nice to us, she'll screw you anyway." The kid didn't mince words, and neither did her mother.

"That isn't why I am being nice to you. And I don't know if you should be talking like that, especially not in front of Violet," he replied.

Her dark eyebrow went up, and instantly, he was reminded of his mother, who would love these quirky kids.

"Violet has heard a lot worse from Mom. Isn't that right, Sera?" Emma turned on her mom, who looked a little shocked at her words.

"Harper said Mommy likes BBSN this morning," Violet answered for her mom, clearly not what her mom would have said, Harrison was sure.

Sera, for her part, chuckled and kissed her daughter's head. "Not quite, baby girl. I corrected Harps this morning too."

"Just the B and the D." Emma rolled her eyes as their order was called. "And I have read *50 Shades of Gray,* so I do know what that means."

"Don't listen then," Sera called as Emma went to get their order.

"Maybe too much information for your kids?" he asked when Emma was out of earshot, though he doubted she was ever not listening.

"She's fifteen, and this one doesn't understand yet."

"Is she supposed to understand at fifteen?"

"She's read the book, Harrison. She understands." Her eyes challenged him, but they were her kids, so it was up to her what they heard.

"So, is it the same Harper as from the engagement party? The one with the best breasts in the group?"

"Yes," she said, but her answer was drowned out by Violet.

"Mom has the best tits in the house. Until I get mine—then I will." She giggled as she patted her chest.

"I get a lot of calls from the school. Way more than with Emmaline." Sera said dryly as she watched an employee bring a tray of drinks and cake.

"I can see that happening," Harrison admitted with a chuckle.

Once the cups were placed and cakes distributed, Violet had to go to the restroom. So, Sera took her with an apology. But Harrison didn't mind; they had nothing that wouldn't keep for a few minutes.

"If you think you're special, you are wrong," Emma said from the table across from him, with her giant coffee and book in her hand.

"I try to think I am special."

"She fucks a lot of guys."

"Do you meet a lot of them?"

"Don't need to. She gets tired of them very quickly."

"Maybe I'm different."

"Nope."

"Do you still want her together with your dad?" He tried to guess why Emma was so angry with him. That was usually the case when parents were divorced.She chuckled before answering. "I've never seen my dad, nor has Violet. And we never will."

"I'm sorry to hear about that." He was still wondering about her unusual marriage. It sounded like the kid's father wasn't the man she was married to.

"He doesn't matter." Emma shrugged.

Suddenly, he recalled himself as a kid, thinking the same thing. They at least had that in common. Except he hadn't thought about his father in those days. Maybe Emma did, and he felt bad for her, though he didn't know if he was ready to step in as a father for her. He was hoping to be a friend, though.

"Do you talk about sex a lot?" He wanted to know, and she wouldn't lie to him.

"Yes, it's a big topic at the house. The big girls are very active, if you know what I mean." She winked at him.

"I know what you mean by active, but who are the big girls?" he asked.

"Ask your girlfriend if you're so close." She had him on that one

Violet came rushing back before Sera slowly returned to the table, putting an end to his semi-unpleasant conversation with Emma. What he had learned from the kid was that anything could come from her mouth, and she was going to surprise him every time.

As her mom had said, Emma couldn't finish the coffee, and Sera carried it back to the silver Jeep he had seen earlier. With the kids loaded up, he pulled Sera into his arms. No way was he not kissing her.

"Are we still on for tomorrow, or can we find time earlier?" he asked.

"Tomorrow. I need to spend time with the girls today, and more time next week. I know it sounds like an excuse for distance, but it's not. Just me needing to spend time with my kids." She sighed and pulled from his arms. He wondered if she thought that it would be a deal-breaker, that she thought he was so shallow that he didn't want to let her have time with her kids.

"I understand. Maybe I could take you all out one night?" He tried to assure her that he wanted to know her kids also and that he knew how important they were to her and wanted to be a part of that.

"Not until after. We have to stop all of this until after," she relaxed and whispered. He could tell she didn't want to leave him either.

"After your investigation clears me." He agreed as he ran this thumb over her cheek. After couldn't come soon enough.

He could tell she wanted to argue with him, but instead, she opened the car door. "Tomorrow."

"See you then," he said as she shut the door. Again, he watched her back out of the parking spot, stop at the street, and drive out of the lot.

The sun was still shining, and he had learned some very interesting things about Sera. She had children, and he seemed to be very okay with that. Never had he thought he wanted to raise someone else's kids, which was why he wouldn't adopt with Veronica. Not that she had pushed that for more than a week, because she had felt the same way.

But these two kids were so very Sera that they naturally felt like just another part of her that he could love. His mind stopped. *No, not love—like.* This was all too new to call love. Way too new.

CHAPTER TWENTY

HARRISON HAD SPENT two hours with Sera's kids, and she had barely been able to restrain herself from yelling that they were actually his kids. How could he not see that? They looked exactly like him; every little thing screamed that his genes were in those girls.

But he had not noticed or thought it was possible or even imagined that it was probable. But she saw it so clearly.

Yesterday when she had shown up at his place in the late afternoon, she expected him to ask her about them. To ask why they looked like him, whose they were, and why she had hidden them from him—and continued to.

But instead, he had pinned her to the wall and had her naked within moments. Nothing meaningful had been said for hours. Not that she was complaining; she hadn't seen him in over a day at that point.

But today was his second HR interview to see if his answers had changed. This morning she had set up a meeting through his new personal assistant, and it was almost time. And right now, she had no idea how she was going to conduct the damn thing.

Talking about Harrison's sex life when it did not include her was going to slowly kill her, but death would still at the end. Before they started their own relationship, it wasn't personal, but now it was very personal to Sera. Knowing what was going to be said and hearing it again was going to be awful.

Before she could chicken out, Harrison strode confidently into the office, very different from the first interview where he had been willing to tell her anything to get the investigation over. Now, he must think she was on her side. But in reality, all her doubts were still there —too many of them.

"Sit down, Harrison. Once again, I need you to answer the questions honestly. Do you want another person present? A male or female?" she asked while opening her file.

"No, I'm fine with just you." He leaned back in the chair.

"Did you want someone else to conduct the interview?" she asked, not liking how relaxed he was.

"No, just you. But since you already know the answers, do we really need to do this?"

His words made her cringe.

"Okay, I'll be asking some of the same questions and some different ones. How long have you been with the company?"

"Ten years. I told you last time," Harrison said like she was wasting his time.

"How long were you married, and when did you get a divorce?" She really didn't think he would answer since she already knew from the last interview and he wasn't happy to be doing another.

"Married since I was twenty and divorced for four. As I told you." His answer was clipped.

Fighting her irritation at him, she went on. She had to get this done. "Did you sleep with other women while you were married?"

"Yes, and so did you, so it doesn't matter." His jaw was set as he crossed his arms.

Taken aback, Sera wondered if he thought she wouldn't do the interview after they had sex? That she would disregard her integrity for a roll in the hay with him? Was it possible that was why he had slept with her? Had she fallen into a trap she hadn't even suspected?

"Have you ever had an affair with someone at work?" She continued.

"Not ever," was all he said, though his anger was palpable. But he had repeated what he had said before they had slept together, which meant his statement was now a lie.

"Have you ever touched anyone inappropriately at the office that you are aware of?" she tried another.

"No, No, No, Sera. I have told you over and over again that she lied about everything. Why can't you believe me? I thought that after this week, you would believe me." His voice had an edge to it, an edge she didn't like at all.

"This is over." She shut her folder. "You may leave. I will have someone else contact you for another interview."

"You finish it." He pointed at her folder.

"Why? You're pissed at me for asking these questions, and you won't give me an honest answer anyway." She shoved the folder into her desk drawer. His anger was now hers.

"I have not lied to you," he stated.

"I can't do the interview. A second has to be done, but I cannot do it," she admitted, more to herself than to him. Why had she thought she could be objective for Harrison Dean? From day one, he could do no wrong in her eyes; even his wrongs had been forgiven. But being on Harrison's side wasn't her job. If he was lying, she was letting down a young woman who had done nothing but what Sera had done: fall for Harrison's lies.

Harrison looked at her intently. "You don't believe me." He leaned toward her. "I can't believe you don't believe me," he said in disbelief.

"I want to believe you, Harrison, but you make it hard." Sera crossed her arms in defense as his anger grew.

Harrison was on his feet, leaning down and looking at her as he whispered, "You woke up in my bed this morning, Lovely. And you have the nerve to tell me you don't believe me?"

"This is not about us, Harrison. This is about me conducting a fair investigation. You're letting our relationship get between that," she whispered back.

FALLING FOR THE SINGE MOM   113

"I just think you should believe me."

"Because I'm sleeping with you? Is that why you slept with me?" She leaned back as if she was seeing him for who he was. He had shown her no interest until she was put in charge of this investigation. Now in a short time, they were lovers. Was he so ruthless to use her just to keep his job? Had she read him so wrong all these years?

"Of course not." He actually looked so shocked at her accusation, she almost believed him. It almost made her forgive him.

"Well, I'm saying now that I will not see you again until this is over. Long over. And Aspen will call you for an interview." Her words came out steadier than she felt. She was completely crushed. Right now, she wished she hadn't left a bag at his place last night for the first time.

"Since you don't believe me, I think that would be best," he agreed and pushed off her desk and headed out the door.

He slammed her door behind him, just like old times. But it was true. She didn't believe him because he had denied that he had ever had a relationship at work. But she was a coworker, and they had been having sex for a week. That answer should have changed because of her, but it hadn't. So, had he lied the entire time? Though he didn't remember their night together all these years later, had he had another affair with someone at work he wasn't willing to talk about? Was it Kylie Nash? Was it more than Kylie Nash?

She had no way of knowing. She hadn't heard from anyone that she had interviewed that he had other affairs, but they had kept it quiet, so others could have also.

She called Aspen, who was happy to conduct the interview, even if Sera hadn't told her why she couldn't do it anymore. And to her credit, Aspen hadn't asked. But now she felt run down and drained. With a quick text, she had three of the girls ready to meet for drinks later in the evening. Yes, she should spend the night with her little girls, but she needed her big girls for this.

CHAPTER TWENTY-ONE

HARRISON WAS willing to admit that he had no right to yell at Sera for not believing him. Other than them sleeping together, he had not given her any more reason to believe him. Then he had blown up at her, and now it was over.

Ending their relationship hadn't ended the investigation or ended the fact that he wanted her in his bed, in his life. Yesterday he had done the interview with Aspen. It had gone well, and he had been able to keep his temper in check. There had even been more questions than Sera had asked in the first interview. Aspen had even been able to get him to expand on his previous answers. Every moment he was being interviewed, he had wanted Sera there with him, beside him. To have her support instead of her suspicions. He could see that after Aspen's interview, he hadn't taken either interview with Sera seriously, just like most work-related talks with Sera.

Aspen had told him that the Kylie Nash interview had gone well and that Sera was making a report about it. The woman hadn't gone into much detail about it, but she had said she was very believable, which didn't bode well for him.

So far, he hadn't seen Sera since the blowup, but he hadn't gone out of his way to see her. Nor had she gone out of her way to see him. This was why he didn't do interoffice romances: the fallout.

At least Wednesday afternoon had passed quickly as he finished his last appointment with Gaines and Marlo Hawthorne. Every year they revised their will. Some years they split their sizable estate between their three children, and sometimes their son got everything. Their daughters never got anything more than twenty-five percent apiece, and typically, like this year, they only got fifteen percent.

Every year it was the same; they came in and signed everything, but their children were never seen or talked about that much. In fact, his office didn't even have addresses for any of the Hawthorne children, which would make distributing the inheritances an issue when the couple actually died.

Marlo sat with her purse on her lap, as if there might be a thief in the building, and waited for the meeting to be done with bored disinterest. Gaines acted like his estate wasn't a tenth of the size it had been the first time he had written the will nine years before. The family money that each had inherited years before was completely gone, as was the estate that they had lived on for most of their marriage. The company that Gaines had inherited and then run into the ground after thirty years had been dispersed years before. They were now left with a condo and a small amount of money that Harrison was unsure if it would last until the couple was dead.

Still, they came in and acted like their three kids should be grateful for the pennies they would receive in a few years. If it were Harrison, he would spend those pennies to find out where their kids were and get them back.

"So that takes care of another year," Harrison said, gathering up the signed documents and putting them in a blue folder. Sera was right; it made him smile at the color.

"And you don't need the children to sign, correct?" Marlo asked, pulling her purse closer as if she could sense he was born poor.

"You can send them here if you see them," he suggested like he did every year. "I will get these completed and send them to you in the mail in a few days."

"The post will lose it," Marlo replied. So far, in nine years, she hadn't said anything that made him think that she had any connection to the real world at all.

"Then you'll have to come back for them." They always did.

Marlo, still hugging her purse, got up and then glared at her husband for not getting up as fast as she had, or maybe at the exact same time. Harrison followed them from the office.

As he reached the outer office, he saw Sera was waiting in the chairs along the wall. His eyes drank in her black skirt and her wavy hair. She was gorgeous today, like every day.

But Sera's eyes were on Marlo Hawthorne. Harrison didn't know what she saw in the older woman, but it made Sera sit up straighter, still holding her green folder.

"Sera?" Gaines was the first to speak.

"Seraphina?" Marlo talked over her husband, her voice controlled.

Sera jumped to her feet, clinching the folder between her hands and bending it as she said, "Mother, Father."

Dumbfounded, Harrison looked at the three of them as they just stared silently at each other. Yes, every year, he allocated Kaine, Arabella, and Seraphina Hawthorne's inheritance, but never had he thought that same person was Seraphina Lovely. He couldn't see her being raised with the kind of money the Hawthorne's had many years before.

"How have you been, Seraphina?" Gaines was the first to get over the shock of seeing their daughter. His eyes actually softened as he looked at her.

Sera, for her part, smiled at her father, but not her usual smile. It was cool and brittle. "You don't really care, do you?"

"I-it would be nice to know," Marlo stammered.

"So, you can tell your friends? Well, I have done nothing for you to brag about, Mother. When I do, I will call." She turned and walked out of the office.

The older couple were still in complete shock as to what had just happened, but it seemed that the bridge-building they had thought could happen with their daughter wasn't going to occur today.

"Does she work here?" Gaines asked in disbelief.

"Yes," Harrison answered, but he wasn't going to tell them much. Based on her response to their question, Sera didn't want them to know.

"Oh god, Gaines, she's a secretary. I knew this would happen. You had to let her go to college," Marlo stated, looking at the door her daughter had just exited.

"I just let her do what she wanted to do," Gaines defended his actions.

"And now she's a secretary!" Marlo couldn't wrap her head around the secretary job.

"Being a secretary isn't all that bad." Beth, his new administrative assistant, added to the conversation. Harrison knew he liked her.

Marlo turned on her in an instant. "Hawthornes are not secretaries."

"Her name is not Hawthorne, ma'am, and she is very good at her job," Beth shot back at the older woman. She too, did not say what Sera's job really was.

There was no way either Harrison or Beth were going to give the couple any further information about Sera, especially if the knowledge would make them want her back simply because of her position. Sera was way more than her job title.

"I don't care," Marlo huffed.

"At least we know where she is for her to sign the will this year." Harrison said as he tried to distract them from obsessing over Sera and her job. Sera was a top executive at the law firm and had been for years.

"Gaines, he'll need to change the will now," Marlo stated to her husband.

"I'll call him later this week, and we can redo it as soon as possible, dear." Harrison was sure the man was going to pat the woman on her head with his condescension.

"We can change it now. We can just tweak a few numbers and print it off. Then we will sign it," Harrison said, ushering the couple back into the office. He shot a smile at Beth, who gave him a thumbs up.

"Good, let's get it done as soon as possible in case something happens to us," Gaines said, as if death was fast approaching.

Watching them settle back on the couch, they looked uncomfortable, nothing like their teenage granddaughter had over the weekend. A granddaughter that they might know nothing about, not to mention Sera's younger one.

He had been in such a hurry to get this done for Sera because she deserved more than the fifteen percent that they were leaving to her. Now that they knew she wasn't rolling in money, they might get it over the twenty-five percent they hadn't surpassed over the years.

"So, what is the split going to be now?"

"The couple looked at each other, and then Gaines said, "No split. Kaine will get it all. The girls are such a disappointment that I couldn't in good conscience leave them anything." His wife nodded enthusiastically in agreement.

Harrison wanted to throw something at the couple. *Who were these people?* They had finally found their daughter, and it meant nothing to them. Nothing at all. Probably because she was only a secretary in their minds. Not worth their time.

Turning away from the computer, Harrison crossed his arms. "I'm going to tell you to kindly find another lawyer. I feel like I cannot continue to represent you because I am friends with Sera's family."

"What?" Gaines stated indignity.

"Sera is my friend, and even if she doesn't know how shitty you're being to her, I do," he explained, getting up from his desk. "Your will from last year will stand until I hear from your new lawyer."

"Well I never," Marlo stated.

"No, Marlo, *I* never. To treat your own child like this. No wonder she doesn't have any contact with you."

"By *our* choice," Gaines argued.

"Has she ever tried to contact you over the years? When her children were born?"

"Of course she would have children, money-hungry children." Marlo put her hand to her heart, not thinking of the lives she had missed knowing.

"I assure you they are not. They're the best kids I have ever met, and I hope they never meet you two." He had to get out of his office and away from them.

Out the door, he smiled at Beth. "Mr. and Mrs. Hawthorne will be leaving soon, and they will be looking for another lawyer when they go. Give them the name of whatever shitty lawyer you can think of. He'll still be better than they deserve."

"Sure thing, boss." Beth didn't even blink an eye at the request, and Harrison was sure she already had an idea of where to send the awful couple.

Down the hallway, he went to Sera's office. Her door was shut, but he didn't hesitate to open it. Letting it shut behind him, he saw she was standing, looking out the window. Her posture was rigid.

"Your parents are shitty people." Harrison wanted to pull her into his arms but held off. He knew she was strong enough to get through this without him. She had before.

"It's been a long time since I saw them. They got old," she said to the window.

"How long?" he asked, his eyes on her stiff back.

"Sixteen years now. Thanksgiving weekend. Turkey, pumpkin pie, and a good old-fashioned disowning."

He still stayed a few feet from her. "Because of Emma?"

From what he knew, the girl was fifteen and a good reason for those two to cut one of their children from their lives. Only they would feel a grandchild was something less than a blessing. If he and Sera ever got together, both of Sera's kids would be smothered in nothing but love by his mom, and she wasn't even their actual grandmother.

"No, not really. I had already decided to marry Bradford. He was beneath me, you see." She finally turned from the window and used finger quotes for beneath. "But Emma was already on the way, although my parents didn't know about her. I've been grateful for that over the years. They don't deserve to know her or Violet."

"Did you think they would come around back then? That they would forgive you for marrying Bradford and want to be a part of your life?" He wondered if there was another side to Gaines and Marlo that he had missed over the years, a forgiving side.

"No, I know Mother. If Bradford was beneath me, so was any child born to him. I have never tried to contact them, and I never will." She shrugged.

"Do you miss them?"

"No. I wouldn't trade a moment of my life today for their money. The only thing I ever learned from them was how to parent. Or how not to parent. I never want to let my girls know if or when I'm disappointed in them. I will support them through everything, always. I raised them with love, not money," she said.

"Your kids are great, Sera. I barely know them and can tell you've done so well with them."

"I think so also. I do sometimes think that I'm the only one who knows how great my girls are."

"Nope, you're not alone. Emma warned me away from you, trying to protect you." He hadn't planned to tell her, but the smile his words caused was worth it.

"She's like me, but don't ever tell her that. She'll be happier when she's older. The teenage years were hard for me also." He could hear the smile in her voice, just talking about her daughter.

"I won't say a word," he replied, wanting to be back in her and her daughters' lives.

"I got the paternity results from Kylie Nash's doctor. That's why I was down at your office. You're not the daddy." She abruptly changed the subject. Was it because they were talking about her kids, and she didn't want him to be a part of their lives? "But the father is a close relative of yours."

"I don't have any relatives. My mother was an only child, and my father's been out of the picture for years," Harrison stated.

"Out of *your* picture, but in someone's." She walked to her desk and opened the crushed file on her desk. "The results said it was possible the father is your first cousin or half-sibling."

"My mother has no other children." He grabbed the file from her hand. He had to see this. Though when he looked at the results, the words made little sense.

"You do have another parent," she said, letting him look it over.

"Not really."

"Well, Jesus, then you're a miracle!" She said sarcastically but wondered about the man who had fathered him and walked away from his life.

"Can I take this to my mom?"

"I can send you a copy. I need the original for my records," she replied as she shuffled through her papers.

"Thanks. I think I'll run out there tonight. What happens now?" he asked.

"Now I'm going to go talk to Kylie again and see what she says about this." She tapped the paper.

"Thanks. I know you didn't have to tell me." It was true—she could have held on to the information. Or she could have sent him an impersonal email about it. After the way he treated her, he would have chosen not to tell her in person.

"You needed to know. This is more than about a lawsuit, Harrison. This is a life." She dropped the folder on her desk.

"I know that, but not a life I helped create." He pointed to the folder as if it were the child itself.

"Not this time," she said and turned back toward the window and looked out at the city.

"Not ever, Sera. Thanks for the reminder." Turning, he stormed out of the office. Somehow, she still didn't believe the results printed on a document in her own file.

When he got back to his office, the Hawthornes were gone. Beth chuckled as she told him what lawyer she had recommended. The man also worked for Rodgers and Associates, but only because he was married to the boss's daughter. The last time he got an important case, he had lost so badly that he hadn't been given another. Harrison couldn't help but laugh as he went back into his office. Sitting in his chair, he looked at the will that was still on his screen. Seraphina's name popped out at him immediately. Seraphina Marlo Hawthorne.

He noticed her birthday had been just two weeks before. Glancing at his calendar, he realized her birthday was the day she had interviewed Kylie Nash for the first time—the day she didn't come back.

She had turned thirty-six, just like she had told him in the car when she was soaking wet and sexy as hell, and he hadn't even known. He assumed her friends had taken her out; they seemed like they'd show her a good time out on the town.

But still, it nagged him that he had missed her birthday, even if it had been before they had started seeing each other. He would have liked to have known.

Closing the file for the eccentric couple that had created Sera Lovely, he was happy she had found a way to raise her kids differently from how she had been raised. Marlo would have died if Sera had brought up her sex life like Emma and Violet had on Saturday. He would take her kids any day over the kind of kids Marlo had tried to raise. All except Sera; she'd turned out perfect.

All he had to do was get past this case so he could prove to Sera that he wanted her just as she was.

CHAPTER TWENTY-TWO

THE CLOCK HAD STRUCK five over a half an hour ago, and Sera was still stuck in her chair, staring out the window and thinking of her past. A past full of the constant disappointment she had caused her parents. Nothing she had ever done was good enough for them.

From dance recitals where she hadn't been able to remember all the moves to getting a B on a report card. She was constantly compared to Juliette, who had died weeks before Seraphina's own birth in a car accident that had also claimed the life of her young nanny. At three, Juliette was forever perfect in her parent's eyes, and Seraphina had been a poor substitute. She'd never reach any level of perfection.

Her only saving grace was that she had been born the same day as Kaine, who had been perfect by virtue of just being male. He had also been great at sports and smart in school. He even had a ton of friends, something Sera never had. All her life, she lived in his shadow, barely a blip on her parents' conscience.

Six years later, they had brought home her replacement: Arabella. Girly and delicate, she was perfect in every way, just like Juliette. From her grace and quiet demeanor, Arabella could do no wrong in her parents' eyes. Never had, as far as Sera could remember.

By her teen years, they had sent Sera to a boarding school to try and improve her grades. She was averaging a disappointing A- most of the time. The years out of the house and away from her parents had taught Sera not to depend on her family; she had herself. Her siblings had been sent to different private schools, and they had lost any sibling connection that might have had.

When Sera had chosen a state school, that had been another major disappointment for her parents. Kaine had chosen a private school that Gaines had attended years before. It didn't matter that the school she had selected was known for its business department, and the employment rates were high. State school was state school, and she, a Hawthorne, was supposed to be better than that.

During her sophomore year, when she realized she was pregnant with Emma, she didn't go to her parents until she already had a solution: to marry Bradford. Her parents had decided that if that was her path, they would let her go and do it without them. At the time, Sera hadn't been surprised by their reaction. After all, she knew her parents.

When Bradford had left and didn't come back, she turned to herself and her new kids to make their family work. It was hard and would have been easier to walk away from the five teenagers who'd barely tolerated her for the first months. By the time Emma had been born, they had all been there, and all had pitched in when needed with the new baby.

She hadn't lied to Harrison when she had said she wouldn't trade the inheritance she walked away from for her kids. She loved all seven of them and couldn't see herself not being their mom. Each child had affected her in their own way, and each had made her a better person by knowing them.

Her parents didn't deserve to know any of her girls because they were all better people than her parents pretended to be.

"Sera?" She heard Harrison's voice from behind her.

Spinning her chair, she turned to look at him. Though she had seen him earlier, her parents had taken all of her attention. Right now she could analyze him in his black suit and silver tie. The only signs that the day had been long and stressful was that his hair was no longer perfectly styled; it was in slight disarray. "What, Harrison?"

"I was heading out to my mother's. Did you want to interview her?" His words surprised her. Was he inviting her to actually interview his mother, or just meet his mother? Because whatever happened last week between them was over. She was pretty sure it was over.

"Do you want me to interview your mother?" she questioned. Interviewing the woman hadn't even crossed her mind. They were a bit biased.

"Maybe you need a character reference for your report." He shrugged. He wanted her to meet his mother; that was obvious now. Maybe it was because he had met her parents and had seen the disaster that she came from. Could he be trying to take her mind off her own childhood?

"I don't know if I should," she hedged. It was the truth.

Her heart told her to jump at the chance to meet her children's grandmother, the only good one that they would ever have. But then she would have to lie to an old lady. A lie by omission, but a lie just the same. Just like with Harrison.

"Just call it a character reference. Please." The pleading at the end caught her by surprise. He had never asked her for something like this before.

"Okay, as a character reference." She grabbed a legal pad and pen, shoved them into her briefcase, and they headed out.

They took Harrison's car, which was still parked in the same parking lot she always parked in. Since he always teased her about her Jeeps, she let him drive. During the drive, she admitted the person who had taught her to fix cars was actually the maintenance man on their estate, not her father at all. As she grew up, she needed to get out of the house more and more, and found herself in the garage, learning about cars from a man who didn't have to waste his time with some rich kid. But he had anyway, which was something Sera had always been grateful for when there wasn't money to fix cars.

Emily Dean lived in a nice little neighborhood. The houses were neither new nor old, and all were taken care of. Though she knew

Harrison hadn't grown up in this house, she could still picture him there, riding his bicycle up and down the sidewalks.

The door opened as Harrison pulled into the driveway, and Sera watched a woman who reminded her of Harrison walk out of the house. After quick introductions, Emily invited them inside for drinks.

The lemonade was tart, and Sera could have gone for a little bit of added alcohol, but she wasn't about to ask the woman. Sera had secrets to keep, and alcohol loosened her lips.

"Sera, it's great to finally meet you. Harrison has told me so much about you." Emily sat down across from her; no lemonade for the older woman.

"I'm at a slight disadvantage. Harrison's told me little about you," Sera said, trying not to stare at the woman who shared so many features with Sera's daughters.

"There isn't much to know. Born and raised here in the city. I really can't see myself living elsewhere." The woman said nothing more, leaving Sera with few details she could share with her children later in life about their paternal grandmother.

"Harrison said you were an artist." Sera tried again, this time with a detail she would never forget.

"Oh, no. I paint, but since I've retired, I can spend more time at it. Are you an artist?"

"No, no, my youngest is the budding artist, and my ..." She bit her lip, stopping herself. Then pushed on. "My stepdaughter is an amazing artist. Hasn't found a way to sell it yet, but one day."

"Two children?" Emily looked over at Harrison in question.

"Well, no, I have seven children. Five from my first marriage, and two that came later." She shrugged. No need to keep it a secret only to have him bolt later.

"Harrison just said two." Emily looked at her son as if he had been keeping things from her.

"My five oldest are now adults, so it's sometimes hard to be their mother. I don't always try," she admitted.

"I know what you mean. Once they get older, you have to let go."

Emily tapped her son's hand as she got up and set a tray of cookies on the table.

"I wish it were that easy. They all still live at home with me. It's nice to have the babysitters, but sometimes it's too many women in one house." Sera chuckled.

"When was I going to meet all these girls?" Harrison asked. He sounded a little miffed at her hiding kids from him again.

"You already have at the engagement party. Everyone but Mabel was there, but Mabel and Lucy are twins and look identical."

"But they didn't look they were much younger than you," Harrison stated.

"I said they were adults," Sera said.

"She did, Harry," His mother agreed with her. "How old are they?"

"Let's see. Bea is twenty-five; we call her Buzz. Agatha is twenty-six, the twins are twenty-eight, and Harper is thirty."

"And you're thirty-six," Harrison pointed out.

"I didn't say I birthed them, Harrison. I said I raised them. When I married Bradford, Harper was fifteen, and I was nineteen, almost twenty." She shrugged.

"That must have been hard being so close in age to them. They must have disliked that. Were you and your husband together long?" Emily asked.

"No, we weren't." She didn't like to tell anyone about her marriage.

"Too bad," Emily said.

"Sera's fifteen-year-old's name is Emma," Harrison pointed out.

"It's Emmaline Rose, but we call her Emma. My youngest is Violet Bianca." She stopped herself—these people had no idea who her children were. No need to go into details. Just because she wanted them to know everything about the girls didn't mean they wanted to know anything.

"Harry said the little one is seven?"

"Yes, she will be eight this fall. I have a spring baby and a fall one. The five big girls are all over the place."

"Harry was born just after Christmas. I hated that I had to buy him a Christmas and birthday present at the same time," Emily said as Harrison shook his head at her.

"Mom, we came because I have a question. The paternity test came back," he edged into the question.

"Harry, if you don't know by now how babies are made, I have failed you." She laughed at his horrified expression.

Sera joined in and raised an eyebrow at him as his face turned red. "No, Mrs. Dean," Sera tried again.

"Oh sweetie, it's just 'miss.' I never married Harrison's father. Lived in sin, yes, but we never married."

"Sorry then, Miss Dean."

"Emily."

"Emily, the test results show that the woman's baby is a close relative of Harrison's. Cousin or half-brother," Sera said causally in case she was stepping into family drama she wasn't aware of.

Emily shook her head. "I didn't have any other kids."

"What about my father?" Harrison asked.

"I don't know. I haven't seen him since you were small. At that time, he had no other kids. But it has to be his side since I have no one on mine," Emily said.

"Harrison said he was created by immaculate conception, so I assumed there was no other side." Sera glanced over at him. He didn't seem to think she was funny.

"He always did think he was special," Emily agreed.

"I've noticed that also." Sera chuckled, falling in love with the woman and seeing a little of each of her girls in her personality.

"As far as I know, Harry Rolf never had any more children. But I haven't seen him in over thirty years now. A lot of time for that kind of stuff." Emily looked at her coffee cup as she spoke.

"Do you have any way we could contact him?" Harrison took his mom's hand in his.

"No, and I don't want to. Nor do I want you to contact him." Emily visibly paled and squeezed her son's hand.

"Okay, Mom, I won't," Harrison said.

"Good. Now I need you to move some stuff around upstairs, if you will excuse us, Sera." Emily jumped up from the table, her ex forgotten with Harrison's promise.

Like a good son, Harrison shrugged off his suit jacket and followed her from the kitchen, rolling his eyes as he went. Now alone, Sera was unable to stay seated as she waited. She needed to discover everything she could find about Harrison and his family.

Maybe because she had just run into her past was the reason why she wanted to know more about Harrison's. In the semi-dark living room, she found pictures. Harrison at his high school graduation, so closely resembling the boy she met two years later. Another of him and Veronica in a professionally posed shot, neither looking overly happy. The one that captivated her was baby Harrison, probably less than a year old, laying on his stomach on a blanket, smiling at the camera. In her bedroom, she had almost an identical picture of Emma doing the same thing, looking the exact same way.

She felt creepy as she snapped a picture of it with her phone, then one of his graduation shot. At this point, the future was unknown, and the girls might want to know what their father looked like one day. At least now she could show them.

Sinking into the closest chair, she wanted to just run away from his house and these people. Harrison and Emily deserved to know about the girls. Sera was just being selfish by keeping them away from them. Emily would love them unconditionally, as would Harrison.

But in fifteen years, Sera had made a life for her girls, a life that would be turned on its ear if she let Harrison and Emily into it—split custody holidays and watching Harrison find love again, without her. Seeing it in the office was going to be hard enough. Seeing it when he took her children away from her for holidays would kill her.

As she stared at the picture of Harrison from when they first met, she knew she hadn't fallen for him in the last few weeks. She had loved him for years. She had maybe not loved him when they'd made Emma, but by the time Violet came, she was in deep.

"Are you okay?" Emily said quietly as she sat in the chair near Sera's and squeezed her knee.

Shaking herself, she said, "Sorry, just lost in thought."

"I understand. He likes you too," Emily whispered.

Swinging her eyes to Harrison's mother, she said, "What?"

"Harry, he likes you also. The last time he was here, he told me about you. And you like him too. Sometimes you have to be told." Emily grinned at her.

"I don't have to be told. I've known for a long time." Sera picked a nonexistent piece of lint from her skirt.

"But he never knew. Harry's been drifting for a few years. Well, more than a few. That woman threw him for a loop." Emily admitted with a nod at the picture of Harrison and Veronica

"You didn't like her?" Sera looked up at the older woman.

"Not even in the beginning," Emily said, shaking her head. "Not that I told Harry. It wouldn't have changed anything if I had. He thought he loved her and that she loved him."

"That happens." Sera had no idea how else to respond to Emily's confession. She had also disliked Veronica instantly.

"How did you raise seven children? One was bad enough." Emily chuckled.

"One day at a time. But I never really mothered the five older ones; they were long past wanting or needing a mother. They needed someone who was there for them no matter what, so I made sure they knew they were loved and wanted and had someplace where they belonged."

SERA LOOKED at the picture of Harrison and his wife. They wore matching shirts and were touching, but the pose seemed forced. "My marriage was not like Harrison's. I married Bradford to have a father for the child I was carrying, and he married me to have a mother for his children. It wasn't a love match; it was convenience. Within a month, he had moved to South America and hasn't returned once."

"Never?" Emily asked in dismay.

"Not even for his kids. So, I started dating about a year after was Emma born. But I stayed married to Bradford until Bea graduated. I couldn't risk any of them going to foster care. That was six years ago.

Neither of my children are Bradford's." Sera wanted the woman to know but didn't say who their father was.

"Harry doesn't know?"

"I usually don't tell people about it. It leads to a lot of questions I don't want to answer. At work, I like people to think I'm still married. It makes it easier." It seemed odd to tell this woman that; in fact, it was odd telling anyone. At first, it was an unconscious thing to not tell, but later she didn't correct people because she didn't want to.

"I can see that. I let people call me Mrs. Dean for years without correcting it," Emily said, and Sera knew she understood.

"What are you two chatting about?" Harrison asked from the doorway. His tie was gone, and even his sleeves were now rolled up.

"Just life, Harry," Emily answered her son as she got up. "How about I make something to eat? It's getting late."

"Sorry, Emily, but I should be getting home soon," Sera said, not wanting to have a meal with people she was lying to.

"Sorry, Mom. We rode together, so I'll have to pass also," Harrison echoed.

After a quick goodbye, they were heading back to the parking lot where Sera's Jeep was. No words had been spoken between them as Harrison drove. Sera didn't know what Harrison was thinking; it could've been anything. Her mind was racing with all the information she had gotten about Harrison and his past, how he had been raised, and how that made him who he was.

Her mind could stop thinking about how he would react to learning the truth about the girls. Or how his mother would react. It was clear to her that family was important to them and that they would embrace her girls. But she was still scared to share them because they had the means to take them from her. Though she was sure they would not, she couldn't take that chance, not yet.

Pulling into the parking lot, Harrison put the car in park but didn't move. Nor did Sera.

Harrison broke the silence between them. "We need to talk."

"Harrison, no." She couldn't talk to him. She had too many secrets that wanted to get out.

"Please, Sera. I'm tired of pretending that I don't miss you and that I don't want you back." He turned and looked at her finally.

"You and I both know it's for the best to just stay away from each other until after the investigation is done." Sera closed her eyes as she spoke. She couldn't look into his eyes.

"But it's done. I'm not the father," he replied earnestly.

"That part is done, but the harassment case is still open. Just because you didn't father her child doesn't mean the rest didn't happen." She finally opened her eyes, which was a mistake because she saw the pain in his.

"You still don't believe me?"

"It isn't what I believe or not. I have to prove or disprove it." The words were the same as she had said before.

"Can you disprove it then?" he hissed.

"I can't talk about it." She opened her door to finally leave.

"Can't or won't, Sera?" he called out to her.

Not answering, she slammed the door shut and walked to her Jeep. He roared off before she even got into the cab, so she sat and thought about everything that had happened that day.

Oddly, they had each met each other's parents in one day—one long, emotional day.

CHAPTER TWENTY-THREE

IT HAD ONLY TAKEN Harrison two blocks for his anger to dissipate and another two blocks to drive back to the parking lot. But Sera was already gone. The white Jeep was no longer in the parking spot. This was the third different Jeep she had driven since he'd met her, but when he had pulled into the parking lot today and saw the vehicle, he had known it was what she had driven today.

With only the knowledge that she lived near the dive bar he had seen her at so many weeks before, he headed in that direction to see if she was there. Maybe she needed a drink after all the emotions of the day. Maybe her friends, or kids, would take her out.

It seemed right that the women who'd catered the party were her stepdaughters. The way she had went out and yelled at Brad and the redhead? That was a mom move. The fact that they were close to the same age would take some getting used to.

The question of who took care of the two little girls when they were together came into focus, and he realized it must be her other kids. Since they all lived together, it wasn't a big deal when she stayed with him all night.

While still at his mom's house, Harrison had hovered in the hallway as Sera and his mom discussed her marriage and why she had stayed with her first husband. It had surprised him to hear that Sera had started dating while Emma was still a baby. But if neither kid was her husband's, then she clearly still felt no loyalty toward him, especially as he had left her anyway.

After driving for half an hour, he slammed on his breaks when he saw six Jeeps of the same vintage as Sera's crowding the driveway and curb of a massive Victorian house. The blue one Sera typically drove was there, as were the red and gray ones he had seen on occasion, along with another red and two white ones. He wasn't three blocks from the bar that he had seen her at so many weeks before.

The front door slammed open as he took in the fleet, and Buzz and a brunette bounded out of the house. Together they climbed into one of the Jeeps on the street and took off, yelling about alcohol and laughing as they went.

He knew he had found Sera's place, but no way was he going into that house if it was still full of women who would probably kill him for hurting their mom. Driving away, he was happy he knew where she was finally but was still heartbroken that it wasn't with him. Tomorrow was soon enough to talk to her and tell her he wanted to try again with a relationship after the investigation was finished.

By morning, Harrison was ready to lay his cards on the table. He wanted her and was willing to wait for her as long as the investigation lasted, as long as she was still willing to let him into her life.

He headed down to her office first thing in the morning but was confronted by a closed door. Was she inside in a meeting, or was she gone? Had she drunk too much the night before and decided not to come into the office?

At noon, the door was still closed, but one of the men in HR told him she had called in sick that morning, which was a lie. She was avoiding him again, but she couldn't stay away forever. She had to come back to work.

CHAPTER TWENTY-FOUR

"ARE you actually cleaning up puke in your work clothes?" Agatha asked, peeking around the bedroom door.

It was just before 8 p.m., and Agatha was still up from the previous night. Her dark hair was standing on end, and there were dark circles under her eyes. Agatha looked like shit, but she still looked a hundred percent better than she had a year before.

Last year, Agatha wouldn't have weighed a hundred pounds carrying a Christmas ham, and now she was filled out in places Sera had never seen on her before. Since she was in high school, she had the most prominent cheekbones of anyone Sera had seen. Now you couldn't even see them.

"Someone has to. Violet's been sick most of the night, and everyone has scattered." Sera couldn't blame them as she tossed the dirty sheet into the clothes basket. She wanted to run away also.

"Flu?" Agatha took a step back from her.

"I think so. I called in, but I have an interview this morning."

"Harassment case?" Agatha asked. Agatha would remember.

"Yes, second with the victim." Sera tossed the fitted sheet on top of the flat in the hamper.

"Want me to go with? I can see shit from a mile away." Agatha folded her arms and leaned against the doorjamb.

"You wouldn't stay awake," Sera countered, knowing Agatha had yet to go to bed after coming home from work at close to dawn. But a second person there wasn't the worst idea in the world. Now that Aspen had left to open her own law firm, Sera was left without a second person. Then Sera's own assistant had called her to say she was also sick, which left her doing this alone.

"To weed through shit I will," Agatha argued.

"Shower and raid my closet. Pretend to be a lawyer. I'll see if I can get someone to watch Violet for a few hours. Oh, and I ask all the questions, got it?" Sera grabbed the laundry basket as Agatha gave her a thumbs up and headed to the bathroom down the hallway.

By the time Agatha was ready, Sera had started the laundry, gotten Lucy to watch Violet, and washed the bathroom floor. She had also changed her own clothes since she smelled overpoweringly of puke.

Sera had just enough time to doubt her impulsive decision to bring Agatha, but it would make the outing quicker since she hated leaving Violet when she was sick. The only difference between Agatha and Sera's assistant was that she trusted Agatha's instincts about people more.

Strictly speaking, she didn't need a second interview. With the paternity test back saying Harrison was not the father, she was sure Kylie's case would crumble if it went to court. For weeks, Sera had been looking for evidence and had found nothing.

"You should be a lawyer," Sera said with Lucy agreeing from the couch as Agatha came down in black slacks and a green cashmere sweater and even heels—low heels, but still heels. Agatha looked more professional than she had ever before.

"No, thank you," Agatha barked at her when she made it to the landing. Under the new layer of sophistication, she was still Agatha.

"Professional, Agatha." Sera pushed her out the door before either one decided that this was a bad idea. If all went well, Kylie would stick to her story, they would be done within an hour, and Sera would just have to write up a report. It wouldn't matter who was with Sera.

Across town, she was once again let into Kylie Nash's apartment, and Kylie's lawyer was already present. After introducing Agatha as a coworker, Sera watched Kylie to make sure she didn't argue that she had never seen Agatha before. But the woman hadn't been at the company long enough to meet everyone.

Once introductions were done, Sera began asking easy questions about employment length and personal history. Then she launched into the harder ones. Or, what would be the harder ones if the younger woman had been lying to her.

"How long was the affair?" Sera read the prewritten question but didn't need the notes; she knew them all.

"Almost from the moment I started at Rodgers. Almost every day, he would say something not office-appropriate to me," Kylie stated, though Sera noted to herself that last time, Kylie had said it began almost a month after she started.

"Do you have a boyfriend?" Agatha asked without looking up. She too had a notebook she was writing on, but she was actually just doodling pictures that only Sera could see.

"No, not in a long time." The younger woman gave a sad look.

"I know how that is. Are you looking? I am every day, but no luck," Agatha lied. Agatha could bullshit with the best of them.

"Sometimes, but I am not really over my ex yet," Kylie confided but didn't name her ex, who could be Harrison for all Sera knew.

"My last one cheated," Agatha tossed out.

"Mine too. With my friend, my best friend." Kylie's eyes filled with tears.

"Sister for me. It hurts," Agatha commiserated. "Was he jealous that you were hooking up with your boss?" Agatha asked. She had taken over the interview, and Sera was letting her do it. Apparently, Kylie was willing to talk to her.

"He was okay with it. In fact, he was the one who said it would be great if it happened. He even pushed for it to happen in the beginning. It was a little weird, but I loved him, so I went with it. But then he wasn't. It was like a switch." Kylie snapped her fingers.

Sera let go of the breath she had been holding. If Kylie's boyfriend was pushing her to have a relationship with Harrison, could Harrison have been the victim? And if he was the victim, why had he never said anything about it?

"I dated a guy like that. He wanted, I mean, *I* wanted, a three-way. But when it came down to it, he was pissed I let another guy touch me. Like it hadn't been his idea," Agatha said with her shit-eating grin.

"It was exactly like that. I wasn't even attracted to Harrison, but Josh wanted me to be."

"Josh Johnson?" Agatha asked like she knew the guy and was just confirming it.

"No, Josh Rolf," Kylie stated, shocking Sera. Rolf was Harrison's dad's last name, which meant that the men might share a father. But did Josh know? He must have if he pushed Kylie to have an affair with Harrison and get pregnant. This entire thing had been planned from the beginning.

"Did you get busy with Harrison" Agatha leaned toward her, drawing her in like only Agatha could.

"No, he's too old. I mean good-looking but old," Kylie said, not realizing she just admitted far too much. Even her lawyer was shocked into silence.

"Why Harrison? I mean, he is *old*," Agatha emphasized.

"Josh. He knew him and had a plan," Kylie replied, and her face immediately paled. Agatha had just gotten her to admit she had lied.

"I think we are done here." Her lawyer started to get up, trying to stop the interview, but he was too late.

"Thank you for your time, Kylie," Sera stated quietly as she pushed Agatha from the apartment. She had everything she needed for her investigation. She knew that she would never learn anything else beyond what she knew right now.

Outside, the sun was brighter, and the air was warmer. A load had been lifted from Sera's shoulders. Neither woman spoke as they got into the car or as Sera pulled away from the curb into traffic.

"You really should have been a lawyer, Ag," Sera complimented her.

"No way. Do you know how much paperwork that involves?" Agatha complained about a job she knew nothing about.

"But you're really good at getting people to be comfortable with you."

"I'm a bartender who has watched every episode of *Law & Order: SVU*. I should get a law degree just for that alone. That one was an easy nut to crack," Agatha said, referring to Kylie.

"When did you know she was lying?"

"When she said, 'office-appropriate.' Someone fed her that line. She doesn't know how to spell office appropriate, much less use it in a sentence."

"I am so glad I brought you."

"Be happy I didn't card her. She isn't old enough to be drinking whiskey for breakfast. Don't tell me you didn't notice her coffee was laced with the stuff. Maybe there was no coffee at all."

"Says the girl who told me at thirteen that if you take two sips from a Coke can, you can refill it with whiskey for the perfect mix," Sera shot back.

"And I stand by that! Why dirty a glass?" Agatha took no offense as her eyes stayed on the road.

Sera lightly punched her in the arm. "Thirteen was the point."

"Your kid is older than that. Do you think she drinks yet?" Agatha asked. It seemed like she wasn't enjoying the girls growing up any more than Sera was.

"A little, but she doesn't go partying with friends, and I don't think she has had sex," Sera said, but really, she had no idea. She didn't want to just ask her like she did with the older girls.

"The oldest Lovely virgin ever!" Agatha laughed.

"Not even the oldest Lovely virgin in this car," Sera shot back.

"God, you were old!"

"Not me, Agatha Christie." She loved to put her kids in their place.

The dark-haired woman looked away from Sera and out the window. She hated her name, as all of Sera's stepdaughters did. They were all named directly after authors: Agatha Christie, Harper Lee,

Beatrix Potter, Lucy Maud Montgomery, and her twin, Mabel Lucie Attwell. Though Mabel was named for an illustrator.

When Sera had first walked into their house, Agatha went by Christie, but once she'd left high school, she had left that name behind. While the others were sometimes called by their long names, as they referred to them, Agatha's was never said. It was taboo to even say it because Agatha never reacted with anger or teasing like the others; she just instantly withdrew within herself. Just like now.

"So, what happens with your baby daddy now?" Agatha didn't look back at her.

Sera knew that this was not about the investigation but about her telling him about the girls. Because once Kylie told the truth, the investigation was over. Now Sera had to decide to tell Harrison about his daughters or not. Then she had to decide whether start an actual relationship with him or not. One hinged on the other.

"I don't know. I half want to tell him, but I don't want to share them. I've never had to share my kids."

"Maybe he doesn't want to share. Maybe he wants the entire package," Agatha said the words Sera hadn't dared to think about.

"No, neither of us are known for their long-term relationships."

"Except his decade-long marriage, and your decade-long lust for him," Agatha pointed out.

"I have not lusted after him for a decade," Sera countered.

"Are you lying to me or to yourself?"

"Shut up."

"Being with this man may be different, Sera, but it might be a better different. A much better different."

"What about you guys? I couldn't ask him to move into the house," Sera stated. It was her home, the one she had chosen to raise her children in. She couldn't see herself leaving it.

"I wouldn't either. But you can leave us, take Emma and Violet, and go. We will have each other, and you will always be our mom."

"But I would miss you all the time."

"And Cliff pissing with the door open?"

"Not that." Sera cringed at the memory, having experienced that one herself more than once.

"Harper waking everyone up at two in the morning with that damn mixer?"

"Maybe that a little." Though she didn't complain, it did happen all the time.

"Emma walking in on Buzz and some guy naked in the living room?"

"Maybe I need to move out anyway." Sera winced. She hadn't even heard about that, and now she wondered how many times the younger girls had seen something similar. Or, more importantly, how many more times it would happen again.

"See? You want out already." Agatha punched her lightly in the shoulder as Sera parked the Jeep.

"I want us all to live together forever," Sera said as Agatha climbed out of the car.

Agatha stuck her head back into the vehicle, her eyes meeting Sera's. "One day, they will all move out, and you will be alone and lonely. Or you could be with Harrison."

With the slam of the door, Sera was alone. Agatha had been right. It was either Harrison or loneliness in Sera's future. If she didn't grab at him now, loneliness would win.

CHAPTER TWENTY-FIVE

FRIDAY WAS a slow day around the office, and all of the partners and executives had filled the conference room to hear the findings from Harrison's sexual harassment suit. They had gathered to sit and listen to the torrid details about his alleged sex life at the office, one that everyone seemed to be willing to accept as truth.

It was early afternoon, and Sera had been in the office all morning, but Harrison hadn't gone to see her. When this meeting had shown up on his schedule yesterday just before 5 p.m., he knew he only had to wait until the end of the day to talk to her. The case would be completely over by then.

It seemed she had not taken the day off but had been out of the office and working on the harassment case. He wondered if she had done it to avoid him.

All he knew for certain was that the baby wasn't his, which he was already certain of. But he was glad that Sera knew also. Her opinion of him was foremost in his mind this week. Or maybe it was just Sera who was foremost in his mind.

She was sitting across the table from him and down three spots. Today she was in a black blouse, which meant the skirt he couldn't see was white. He loved that outfit of hers because her ass in white was amazing. Her tits in black were nothing but amazing also.

On the far end of the table, Kylie Nash's chair was empty, but her lawyer was there. Both the lawyer and Sera were organizing papers and not talking to anyone else in the room. Each seemed intent on ignoring everything around them as the minutes ticked slowly to the start of the meeting.

"I think we are all here since Miss Nash is not coming," Keith Davidson stated looking around the table. It seemed he was in charge of the proceedings, and since he had demanded the internal investigation, it seemed only right. The old man was pretty smug about the entire thing, considering he hadn't had to face any of the women who had worked in his office over the years. The ones who lasted a month or two had fled, no questions asked.

"No, she isn't," Kylie's lawyer stated quietly. She knew her client should have been there. Everyone in the room knew she should have been there.

"So, I think that we will start with Sera today. She has the answers." Keith shot her a grin, one she didn't return as she opened her perfectly straight blue file.

"I just want to start today by saying that this company has been lucky that these types of lawsuits are not coming at us every day." Her words were directed at everyone in the room, but mostly toward him. "This company has a no-fraternizing clause in their employee handbook, and with so many more men than women in executive and senior levels, it is easy to see where men could easily wield power over a subordinate woman."

"Th-this isn't about the company, Miss Lovely," Keith stammered.

"It should be, Keith. You are circling the wagons around a man who had power and authority over a young woman who had no recourse if he'd actually done the things she had accused him of." Sera looked down at her folder.

"So, is he guilty?" Miles Craig, another partner, demanded.

Sera turned to him. "Of what, Miles?"

"Of having sex with a woman in this office."

"It doesn't matter because this company has no rules against it, but from my research, he didn't have sex with Kylie Nash. But he has had sex in this office, but then again, so have you," she stated coolly, without emotion. Miles blushed and turned away instantly.

Her words had exonerated him even as she included a dig at the partner's morals, but the lie she had told about him angered him instantly. He had never had sex here, ever. He had told her that, but she had never believed it.

"This isn't about me!" Miles huffed.

"Since the baby isn't his, this is over, right?" Keith's voice was quiet as he asked, not wanting to draw attention to himself.

"Yes, because he cannot have a baby. There's no proof that he did it," another partner stated from down the table. Harrison couldn't be sure who it was but thought it might have been Grant Miller.

"Tests can lie, gentleman, and a lack of paternity meant nothing in this case. Low sperm count doesn't mean you cannot father a child. Don't use that as your defense," Sera stated, tapping her pen.

"But is he guilty?" Miles asked from his chair.

"Miles, in reality, my investigation was never going to find Harrison guilty of any of the crimes he has been accused of. Not one of these incidents is against Rodgers and Associates' policy at this point. As of this morning, the lawsuit has been dropped completely. Mr. Dean may or may not be guilty of crimes, but what needs to happen before this happens again is an entire overhaul of the company policy," Sera said.

Had she just brushed over the fact that the lawsuit was dropped? Couldn't she have called him this morning with that information? Did he have to find out with everyone else at this meeting? Did there even have to be a meeting? Couldn't this have not even happened?

All he knew was that she didn't believe him or trust him. Whatever she had thought about him and the events that took place were set the moment the investigation started. Her mind had never wavered.

"We are doing just fine," Keith replied in a condescending tone.

"No, Keith, we are not. This company has left the door wide open for this kind of lawsuit. If this one hadn't been dropped today, Harrison could have been found guilty whether he was truly guilty or not. These are he-said-she-said issues. Without the company to back the accused or the victim, we are no help to either one. If we have a policy in place and trainings on how to implement it, we will safe-guard the company and its employees." Sera closed her file. She was done with this.

"We do *not* have an issue!" Miles stated loudly to a few nods of agreement. A few too many nods.

"Did you want me to start with the issues, Miles? The ones from your office?" Sera shot him a look that had him shrinking back in his chair, hiding. "Starting Monday, I will begin working on getting a policy that will put in place procedures and steps to make workplace harassment something that will never happen at this company again. It will be safe for everyone from partners to paralegals, something that should have been done long ago. And if anyone doesn't want me to do that, ask yourself why. And also, I will walk away from this company I have been at for longer than most of you, and I won't be afraid to say why."

Sera got up, looked everyone but Harrison in the eye, and walked out of the conference room with her head held high.

The room was silent for half a beat before Miles stated, "Good job, son. You beat this one."

"Doesn't really feel like a win," Harrison mumbled.

"But it is. Now what to do about Sera Lovely." Miles turned to the room.

"Nothing," Harrison stated more confidently. "Sera is right. If Kylie Nash had the proper channels to go through, it wouldn't have gotten this far. It would have been looked at instantly."

"So, you *were* sleeping with her?" Keith asked as if he would be willing to tell all the details now that the investigation was over.

"No, but it would've been nice to have a file that showed no record of harassment," Harrison said.

"But what about us being accused of that?" Keith asked the room.

"Keep your hands off women and your mouth shut, and you

shouldn't have an issue. Or just retire if you can't. Sera is right—the next one will be bad. We lucked out this time with Kylie dropping the suit. If this had gone to trial, it would have brought a lot of bad publicity to Rodgers and Associates." Harrison wondered if his defense of Sera would be enough.

He knew she was right. No matter what Sera had found, he would have lost. In he-said-she-said cases, the victims won every time. Sera could have walked into this meeting and said anything; her investigation meant nothing. If the lawsuit had gone to court, he would've been done.

"What choice do we have?" Miles asked the room.

"Not a one," Harrison answered for everyone.

Keith shot Miles a look. "I guess we let her do it. I told you not to hire her."

"We needed women in the executive branch, Keith."

"See what that got us?"

Harrison stopped listening as he left the room. After all he had gone through, he understood that the company had to change. And it had to change right away.

At least Sera was going to be in charge of it.

CHAPTER TWENTY-SIX

As she cleaned off her desk, Sera was still trying to control the shaking that had started during her meeting with the board. They were still in there, probably discussing her because she had stepped way over the line this time. They were sure to fire her on Monday, if not before. But she stood by what she had said; things had to change.

Sadly, she had said out loud that Harrison had had sex in the office after the countless times he had said he hadn't. It wasn't relevant, and she wasn't going to bring it up, but Miles had pissed her off. She had slipped up.

Sera grabbed her briefcase to leave just as Dawn stuck her head in the door. "Sera, you have a phone call. He says it's important."

"Sure." Sera went back to her desk and picked up the phone, hoping she wouldn't need her computer as she'd already turned it off. "Sera Lovely, Director of Human Resources."

"Ms. Lovely, this is Simon Aldon. I have a few questions for you," a voice stated.

"Sure, go ahead." Shifting the received to her other ear, Sera moved files on her desk to clear it off.

"Are you Seraphina Hawthorne? Daughter to Gaines and Marlo Hawthorne?" he asked.

"That I am, but I can assure you that they have spent years trying to forget I exist." She shoved files in her filing cabinet, not caring if they were organized or not.

"I represent the Hawthornes and am helping them prepare their will. I would like you to come to my office and fill out some paperwork in regard to that." His voice was smooth and self-important.

"I really don't think so, Mr. Aldon. My parents have no interest to me, and I'm not interested in them."

He dismissed her refusal and continued, "I just need you to sign off on the will."

"Why? I've never had to do that before. Why suddenly now?" She wondered why this lawyer was working so hard to get her to sign something. How worried were her parents about her getting any of their money?

"My clients are concerned that you will contest any will that they have prepared."

"I will not. I have no interest in their money or anything else that they have."

"My clients need to make sure that your issuance will not make any claims on their estate either."

"You mean their grandchildren? Most people don't call their grand-children 'issuance.' Then again, most people love their grandchildren. My *issuance* have no interest in my parents' money. In fact, they don't even know that my parents have money or even that I have parents. We have been happy without Hawthorn money and will remain happy without it."

"I will still need you to fill out the forms."

"I know for a fact you don't need me to fill out any forms. I will not get in the way of Kaine and Arabella's inheritance."

"My clients are leaving their money to a charity," he said, avoiding the topic of her siblings.

"Why not Kaine and Arabella?" she pushed. She had always assumed they were with her parents. Why wouldn't they be? Their parents loved them.

"I also need to contact them about filling out a form about their issuance."

All this time, she assumed her brother and sister were still a part of her parents' lives. Never had she thought they would do something that would also get them disowned, not after she had shown them that it was possible. When had that happened? How would she even find them? Would they want to be found?

"When you do, call me, and I will come in and fill out the forms. Until then, just forget I exist."

"I can't—"

Sera hung up on him.

The one nice thing about working with lawyers was that she didn't have far to go if she needed one. If her parents' lawyer called her back, she would get one from the office on the line with her. She wasn't signing anything. Not that she wanted their money, but it would serve her parents right if they had to leave her something. Then the girls would get to go to college on their grandparents' tab.

Sera decided to head out of the office. She couldn't stay there any longer. A long weekend was exactly what she needed. Monday would come soon enough to find out if she had a job. She made it to the parking lot, only to realize she'd forgotten her briefcase by her desk. So much for getting a head start on the harassment policy this weekend.

She made it into the house across town and found all of her girls were already home, which was early for a Friday afternoon. The curtains were pulled, and the TV was on, though they were all looking at her. She was never home on a Friday afternoon.

"Hey, Mom. Tough day?" Mabel asked.

"Shitshow." She kicked off her heels and let them land wherever in the pile of shoes that had collected in the last week since she had cleaned.

"Buzzy, Mom needs a drink," Harper stated and pushed her little sister off the couch.

Buzz got up and backed out of the room. "Wine, beer, something hard?"

"Did you have your big meeting today? The one throwing Harrison under the bus?" Agatha asked from her corner.

"Yes, it was as bad as I thought it would be. Old men are the worst," Sera said.

"That's why I never date old men, that and the gross factor," Lucy replied and held up her bottle to Mabel beside her for a cheers but didn't get one.

"Speaking of old men, where is yours?" Harper asked.

"Old man? He is six years older than you, you brat," Sera said as Buzz came back into the room, her arms full of alcohol. Carefully she set the bottles on the coffee table and waved over them.

"Let me get changed, and I will pick then," Sera stated, wanting to be comfortable when she got drunk. It was always better that way.

"Okay, but hurry back," Agatha said. "Oh, and you got a call on the home phone, which I didn't know we still had, but anyway. A Simon-something wants you to call him about your mom and dad. Very vague and intriguing."

"It's nothing."

"Making it even more intriguing." Agatha raised an eyebrow.

"When did you get parents? I don't remember grandparents at Christmas, not once. Did they just send a card with cash, and you kept it? Mean, Sera, very mean." Buzz took her time picking a beverage and flopped onto the couch with her wine cooler.

"But you have no family," Harper said in shock.

"Yes, I do. Parents and a brother and a sister. I've just been estranged from them for years." She turned to leave.

"Do we ever get to meet Grandpa and Grandma? Wow, I can barely say those words. Grandpa and Grandma," Mabel said slower the second time.

"I prefer Papa and Nana," Buzz cut in and took a drink of her wine cooler.

"No, you will not. They are nothing to us. Same as always," she replied, and then they started to fight about rewinding the movie that had kept playing while they were talking and now had to be rewatched. Or at least some thought so.

Sera chucked as she went and changed for the evening. It seemed like it would be a night in with her kids. It was just what she needed, every one of them around her, distracting her.

She headed back downstairs after shedding her work clothes for jeans and a fun gray Grand Cannon T-shirt. This time, she could smell the lasagna when she made it to the first floor. Perfect.

Sera decided to leave her phone in her room. Harrison had called four times, but she wasn't ready to call him back. After today, she didn't need him yelling at her or tell her it was over. She had known when she went into the meeting today that their relationship was over.

CHAPTER TWENTY-SEVEN

HARRISON HAD BEEN TRYING for over an hour to call Sera, but she had yet to answer. She couldn't avoid him forever, she had to come back to work, but that was on Monday. Harrison couldn't wait to speak to her until then. He knew where she lived now and he would battle every one of her girls if he had to just to speak with her today.

He parked behind a white Jeep and knew that most, if not all, were in the house based on the number of vehicles in the driveway and on the street. There was no way around it. If he wanted to talk to her, he had to go through them.

On the front porch, he could already hear them yelling from inside. Behind the door, he couldn't distinguish if Sera was yelling or not, but a lot of women were. Then they all stopped, and he could hear laughing.

When his knock went unanswered, he opened the door and stepped right into the lion's den, or lionesses' den, as the case may be. Nobody seemed to notice his arrival as he took in the scene. The blonde, Harper, had a brunette pinned to the ground, with the help of Buzz, the redhead. But the brunette was fighting with everything in her.

"Say it, Maby! Say it!" Harper demanded. Harper, the head chef from the engagement party. Harper, who seemed so professional and straightlaced.

"Never, Harper Lee!" the brunette fought back and yelled.

"Just a number, Mabel Lucie," the redhead said.

"I can help you, Maby. Just admit I'm the cuter twin," said a brunette who looked exactly like the one pinned to the floor. She was in a relaxed position on the couch, with a drink in her hand.

As if Harper suddenly had superhuman strength, she threw off the blonde who hit the floor with a thud and pulled away from the redhead. But then Harper's eyes landed on Harrison and became distracted. Her twin immediately took her to the ground again, drink still in her hand.

"Who are you?" she huffed out from her spot under her sister. All eyes turn to him.

"He's Mom's guy," Emma said dismissively from her place on the corner of the couch. He hadn't even noticed her sitting there.

"Oh, the guy from the party. Is he the same one you guys went to coffee with? Sweet," Harper replied and sat down by Emma and hugged her.

"Sera's getting more wine or beer or something," the twin sitting on top of Harper said. She was thrown to the ground by Harper, and she finally spilled her drink all over her shirt, which she then looked at in annoyance.

Harper yelped from her spot on the floor. "Maby, you're an ass!"

"Play the movie again, Em. Maby isn't talking."

"Mom isn't here." Emma looked around the room.

"Mom has company. She can watch it later," a black-haired woman said. Violet was perched on her lap.

Emma shrugged and hit play. The cartoon princess that had been stuck mid-song on the screen resumed her singing. Apparently, the entire group was watching a movie geared toward the littlest of them.

"Timer has a half an hour on it, Luce. I could only find these boxes." Sera walked back into the living room holding up the wine with a smile. She caught sight of Harrison, and her face fell.

"You have company." Emma pointed to Harrison unnecessarily.

"He can leave. We have nothing to talk about." She lowered the wine boxes.

"Those are the *best* conversations," one of the twins said, though he couldn't tell which one. They looked so alike, especially when sitting beside each other. Oddly neither had a wet shirt on anymore. When had the drenched twin changed?

"I'm not leaving until I talk to you," Harrison said. No matter what happened, he wasn't leaving here without having his say.

"Sounds persistent, Mom." Buzz grinned.

"Do we have to call him dad?" one of the brunettes asked sarcastically, earning them both a scowl.

"I'll put them in the kitchen then." Sera waved the boxes in her arms. "We can talk in there, without these jerks listening."

"Wait, mom," the blonde called to her.

Sera turned back.

"Leave a box and tell us when Maby had her first experience. Buzz says she was twenty-two, and I say it hasn't happened yet." Harper shot her sister a look and stuck out her tongue.

Sera rolled her eyes and put both the boxes on the coffee table. "If Maby doesn't want you guys to know, I'm not telling you either." She pointed at Harper.

A throw pillow flew past her head as Emma said, "That was not an answer."

"The only one I'm giving you bastards," Sera replied and turned from the group.

In the kitchen, he was surprised at how big the room was, but still somehow cozy at the same time. Sera leaned against the kitchen cabinet as far from him as she could get. Her body was rigid when she asked, "What are you doing here?"

"Where did you go after the meeting?" With a few steps, he cut the room between them in half, hating the distance between them.

"It doesn't matter to you. Now how do you know where I live?"

"You live by the Grog, and your house is surrounded by Jeeps. It didn't take long once I started looking." He took another step closer to her. No way was he mentioning that he had searched her out before today. That today, all he had to do was drive straight here to find her. He took another step towards her, and still, she didn't move. "Why didn't you answer my calls?"

"I didn't need your anger today." Sera's arms crossed over her gray T-shirt. Harrison noticed it was almost the exact same outfit she had worn to the office the Saturday he had met her girls. Just a different color.

"I got over being angry, Sera. You were right. A court trial wouldn't have ended pretty, whether I was innocent or not. There was no way I could prove or disprove any of it. I couldn't even convince you I didn't do what Kylie said I did."

"I know you didn't do it, Harrison. You said you didn't, and I believed you. I didn't need Kylie's story to fall apart for me to believe you, but for the investigation, it was nice to have Agatha trip up Kylie on Thursday morning."

"Agatha? Your daughter?" He looked toward the living room, though he couldn't see any of the women from where he was standing.

"I needed a second person. Aspen has left the company, and Violet was sick all night, so I wasn't going into the office that day. Agatha can get people to talk when she wants to," Sera said.

"When did you believe me?" he asked as Harper came into the room.

"I need to make garlic bread, Sera. Move your convo somewhere else." Harper started taking out the ingredients ... loudly.

With that, Sera led him through the house again. This time nobody looked away from the TV as they went up the stairs. Well, nobody but a pair of little blue eyes sitting on her older sister's lap. He waved at Violet, and she waved back.

At the top of the stairs, she led him down a short hallway and into a bedroom. Why he was surprised that it was her bedroom, he didn't know. It was her house, after all.

The room was small compared to his, but what his was missing was the wall of pictures Sera had collected of the girls growing up. He could easily pick out who was who in most pictures, even if he didn't know them well. The difference from girl to girl had always been there.

"I believed you the moment you denied it. Why would you lie? There are no rules against sleeping with your coworker." She closed the door behind her and started to move across the room.

"But I've never slept with a coworker before." Removing his jacket, he turned from the wall to watch her pacing. Her blue jeans were tight across her ass.

"You slept with me, and I'm a coworker. You lied about that during our last interview. You still were denying you had done that." She stopped and folded her arms.

"We hadn't been sleeping together before. I don't know who said I was, but they are lying." He had no idea who could be the liar. Somehow, this entire thing came down to her thinking he'd had sex in the office still.

"No, you—maybe you just don't remember it happening," she stammered, not sounding too convinced about it. Maybe he was getting through to her.

"I would remember *that*. When did they say it was?" Harrison tossed his jacket on her bed. He was going to get to the bottom of this tonight.

"Years ago. Many years ago."

"Please, Sera, just tell me the name. I'll talk to them. They must be mistaken. It wasn't me." He knew it was a mistake, a mistake that was getting between them.

"There's no mistake," she asserted, her back stiffening.

"Damn it, Sera, whoever it is, they're lying to you!" He pulled off his tie and tossed it on his jacket.

"I am not a damn liar, Harrison. I know what happened, even if you don't remember." Her eyes were full of anger.

"I didn't call you a liar." He wanted to pull her into his arms and make the anger go away.

"Yes, you did. I didn't have to have a damn informant, Harrison, it was *me*. You slept with me." He could see her fingernails digging into her arms.

"No way. That did not happen." He would have remembered if they had slept together. No way could he have forgotten sleeping with Sera Lovely; she was unforgettable.

"You were drunk at a Christmas party, and it happened on the couch. The couch you hate and don't even sit on." She bit her lip, and her nails dug in deeper.

Nothing came to him, nothing at all. His divorce had been bad and long. He couldn't remember a Christmas where he and Veronica weren't together. Shaking his head, he had no clear idea of when Sera was referring to.

"If I hated it so much, I would get rid of it. I've always liked that couch. It brings character to a boring office."

When everyone had boring uncomfortable chairs to sit on, he offered his clients a place to relax, to not feel like being in his office was worse than going to the dentist for a root canal. His hope was that his clients would have a better experience because of it.

He turned to her wall of pictures again. One caught his eyes instantly because he had seen it before. It was him lying on the floor as an infant, smiling at the camera, but this picture was brighter, and the blanket was yellow and not blue.

Pulling it off the wall, he looked at it closer, as if holding the photo would tell him more about it. "Why didn't you believe the paternity test results I sent you?"

"They had no bearing on the paternity test. You had to take it and get the results anyway." She was looking at the picture he held. She had seen all of his pictures in his mother's living room. This was almost an exact copy of that photo. Why was it even here?

"Why didn't you believe the test results?" he asked again, sitting on the end of the bed, unable to look away from the picture.

"Because you got me pregnant a year after the tests were taken," she admitted what he couldn't bring himself to believe.

"Violet is mine? Why didn't you tell me? Didn't you think I deserved to know?" He looked at the familiar blue eyes, the dark hair. His daughter, a daughter he had been denied her entire life.

"You were still married and were working on staying married. I was still married also. And you didn't remember that night, none of it." Her words came out in an anguished rush, but her explanation sounded legitimate.

"And now, more recently? After I had met her? After I had fallen in love with you?" He tried not to be hurt or angry about what she had done, but it was hard.

"She's been my baby for all these years, and I wasn't ready to share her. But I did feel very guilty about it. I didn't know if you would believe me." She walked away from him finally, no longer looking at the picture in his hands.

His eyes went to the wall and looked for more pictures of Violet, of his daughter. "When's her birthday?"

"September twenty-fourth. She was born in the evening. It was an easy birth, and she was a great baby. Never any trouble." Sera sat on the bed.

"I have a daughter," he said the words out loud, testing them because it was hard to believe the words were true.

"Harrison, can I see the picture you're holding?" she asked, pulling his attention away from the wall with his daughter's pictures on it. He could pick out Violet in another and another as she grew up. His daughter was downstairs watching a movie with her sisters, completely unaware of who he was.

Taking the picture from him, she worked to take the picture from the frame. Once out, she handed it back to him. The photo felt delicate out of the frame. He wanted to put it back in so it would be safe again. So he wouldn't destroy it by accident.

"Look at the back," she whispered.

Turning it over, he read the words that made no sense to him. "Emmaline, nine months."

"Emmaline is yours also. We met in college, during a class on Shakespeare. You dropped the class after two meetings. But after that second class, we slept together. I got pregnant. At that time, I had no idea who you were and was never able to find you again. I tried that time, but failed," she admitted.

"I remember you," he said, looking at the woman on the bed. He had gone to the wrong class twice, then couldn't remember where it had been. Not that he had tried, really. The only good thing about that class had been the girl who'd sat next to him. Unfortunately, he had been nineteen and had gotten what he wanted from her, and she had been mostly forgotten. All these years later, he couldn't remember anything but her first name: Sara. Then he had met Veronica and stopped thinking about her completely. Until right now.

"I don't expect you to remember me. It was one time, and that's okay. I know you'll want paternity tests for both of them, and I am okay with that as well. You deserve to know them, but just don't take them from me. They're my life." Her voice cracked with her words. She was scared he would do just that. That he would take the children she had raised on her own.

Tossing the picture on the bed, he squatted down and took her hands. "I will never take your kids from you, Sera, but I want to be a part of their lives. I want to be a part of your life. I was waiting for the lawsuit to be over before I asked you to move in with me, but now I think I'll demand it. You *and* the girls."

"You don't have to say that, Harrison. I won't stop you from seeing your kids, so you don't have to make promises you can't keep. And I have the big girls to think about." Her eyes wouldn't meet his.

His heart fell at her words. She was truly scared that he'd take the girls from her. He wanted more than her—their kids; he wanted her. Before he could tell her that, there was a knock on the door. A little voice said, "Mommy, supper's ready."

"Come in, baby girl." Sera's voice had gone from barely there with pain to light and happy in an instant.

Violet immediately bounded into the room. Her jeans were dirty, her pink shirt said 'princess' on it, and her feet were bare. She threw herself into Sera's arms as if she knew her mom needed a hug from her. Sera's arms went around her, and she kissed the dark curly hair that looked like it needed brushing.

"Mommy, you are sad. Why are you so sad?" the girl said, even if her mom was smiling.

"I'm okay, baby girl. How are you?" Sera hugged her again.

"My movie is over, and now it's Harper's turn. She likes scary movies, but she might pick my second-choice movie if I eat everything on my plate at supper. Which I will, because I'm starving," Violet explained with a giggle.

"Harper is nice."

"She is, but she can be a bitch sometimes," his daughter said without missing a beat, which made him smile. This was going to take some getting used to.

"She made lasagna." Sera told the little girl and kissed her forehead.

Violet pulled away and wiped a tear from her mom's cheek, "Lucy did, but she made garlic bread."

Harrison's heart was lost in that instant to his new daughter. The girl was her mom all over again, though she looked so much like him. How he hadn't seen it when he had first met them, he didn't know. It was so obvious now.

"Violet, do you remember Harrison?"

"Yep. He said he'd buy me anything at the coffee shop. Agatha said that I can like you because you make Mom happy." She'd turned to him as she said to him, and he realized he had been discussed at some point.

"You can like him even if he doesn't make me happy." Sera kissed her daughter on the head again, her eyes closed.

"Nope. Only if you like him." Violet pushed herself off her mom's lap finally. "If he is staying, I will introduce everyone."

"I'm staying," he said in amazement. This kid had no fear.

"Okay." She grinned and took his hand.

Holding the tiny hand of the person he and Sera had created, he realized he had no fear of what life with his kids was going to be like. It was like he had been waiting for this moment, this opportunity, for years. The trying and trying with Veronica hadn't taken because his kids were right here, just waiting for him to find them.

On the steps, Violet continued to talk. "Do you want to go in alphabetical order or by age?"

"Age," he answered. He wanted to know that order. But really, he wanted to know everything about them. They were a part of the woman he loved, even if she hadn't given them life. But maybe in a small way, she had.

"Oldest to youngest or youngest to oldest?" Violet continued with the questions.

"Oldest to youngest, and an interesting fact about each one." He threw out, a small challenge that he was sure Violet was up to.

At the landing, he noticed Sera was walking a few steps behind them, watching them and making sure everything was okay for both him and her daughter ... their daughter.

Once inside the warm, garlic-scented kitchen, he saw that everyone was already at the table, and everyone was watching him. All of them wore T-shirts and studied expressions of disinterest.

Violet stopped and turned to him, raising her arms because she wanted him to hold her. Surprised she wanted him to hold her, Harrison picked her up. But inside, he was delighted.

"Okay. Harper is the oldest. She is a chef, but she is not a rat." Violet pointed to the blonde in a yellow T-shirt who waved.

"From the movie, *Ratatouille*," Harper said in perfect French and grinned at her little sister. "I also am very bossy, right, Violet?"

"She is, and she gets mad if you don't move fast enough." Violet giggled.

"The twins are next, but Maby is older. Maby is also smarter than everyone else."

"See, I told you all!" The brunette stood up and bowed at all her sisters before sitting back down. "Violet said it, so it is true."

"Violet is seven. When she's older, she'll realize you are just as dumb as the rest of us, just with a fancy degree," Harper said as she picked at the lasagna.

"Fancy! Can you even say 'masters,' Harper? *Masters*." Maby said the last word very slowly.

"I don't need to, Mabel Lucie. I can say 'own my own business.' *Catering*," said Harper very slowly.

"You share the business with Lucy, Harper," Maby replied, still willing to argue about it.

"So what? We have a company that we built ourselves. What have you done? Oh wait, I know. Went to school forever," Maby's twin chimed in from across the table. They looked exactly alike, even down to the gray T-shirts and ponytails.

"Stop fighting, girls. Let Violet finish," Sera said from beside Harrison as she dished up a small plate of food for Violet. All the women fell silent, though they continued to make faces at each other that he was sure Sera saw but ignored.

"Lucy Maud works with Harper and Maby's twin, but they do not look alike, so you won't mix them up." Violet then whispered, "A hint is that Lucy has a scar."

"Right here." The twin in question held up her arm and pointed to something on it. "Maby stabbed me when we were twelve."

"That is not true. You crashed our bikes together when we were twelve." Her twin argued.

"You said your bike was stronger than mine. I think I won that battle."

"You said you could ride your bike off the roof of the garage, and you landed on my bike. I wasn't even home!" Maby argued.

"Off the garage?!" Sera repeated from behind him. This was obviously something she hadn't known before.

"No big deal. I was there, and we all survived," the redhead said from across the table, not even looking up from her food.

"Says the one who almost killed us all." The dark-haired one pointed to her.

"One small kitchen fire does not kill everyone," Bea said, finally looking up.

"What were you doing anyway? It was three in the morning!" Harper asked in curiosity, but it seemed everyone knew the story already.

"I was making soup." She shrugged.

"How did your bra end up on a burner?"

"It was my sweatshirt and bra. I had some help making soup." She wrinkled her nose.

"And why didn't you smell the smoke?"

At the question, the redhead grinned at everyone. "Because Greg Nichols can give one hell of an orgasm."

Half the room groaned at the revelation. It seemed they all knew the guy. Harrison now knew exactly why Emma had talked about sex so easily.

"Greg Nichols?! You said you never had sex with him!" Lucy nearly stood up as she threw her fork on her plate and glared at her sister.

"I didn't. There was a small fire that got in the way." Buzz waved at the stove.

"To everyone adding him to your list, he is not good at giving orgasms. Not good *at all*," Lucy said, stabbing at her lasagna.

"What ever happened to him?" Harper asked.

"Moved away senior year. I haven't heard anything about him since," Maby answered.

"Now I see why the orgasm was so good. You were twelve." Lucy pointed to the redhead.

"Fifteen, thank you very much," Buzz scoffed.

Harrison looked over at Sera; it was something most mothers would have a reaction to. But she just kept dishing up the lasagna as if the girls were talking about the weather, which either meant she didn't care to much, or that it was nothing she didn't already know. He was sure she already knew the information.

"We're all sticking with twelve," the dark-haired one said with a smirk.

Amid her sister's laughter, Violet resumed her introductions. "Agatha is next, and she is an artist. She watches me after school every day." The dark-haired one waved, and his daughter rested her head against his shoulder as she talked. This was clearly her favorite sister.

"Violet is an artist too," Agatha said, a fact that he had forgotten from their coffee date. His mom was going to be excited to have a granddaughter who is artistic. Well, the woman was going to be ecstatic to have two granddaughters any way she could get them, but it seemed like she was going to be getting seven.

"Buzzy is the baby, but you have to call her Bea." Violet pointed at the redhead, who pushed her plate away from her and turned her full attention to him.

"I am a reporter for the *Times*. If you have any leads on a juicy story, please call me. Please." The redhead grinned. "And you can call me Buzz if you're going to be my dad."

"Oh god!" Emma moaned from beside Buzz.

"Relax, Em, He can be your daddy too." Buzz punched the younger girl in the arm.

"Do not call him 'daddy,' Buzz. That is disgusting," Lucy said from across the table.

Buzz's eyebrow wiggled. "Maybe only when he gives me presents."

Harper started choking on something, and most of the others started to laugh. These women were going to take some getting used to.

"Violet, go sit at the table." Sera handed her a plate once the little girl had slid to the floor again.

"You already know Emma, so I didn't introduce her. She is addicted to vampires." Violet said about her sister and walked away.

The table erupted into a heated battle over vampires and were-wolves. Violet calmly walked toward the group and Maby pushed an empty chair out from under the table for her and helped her into her seat, even as she continued to yell at her sisters.

"Dish up your own, Harrison. I am not your mother." Sera nodded at the food.

Oddly, he realized he was the only one in the room that was not her kid. Filling his plate, he half watched Sera walk to the table where shifting took place, and she was able to sit down next to Violet. An empty chair materialized on the other side of her, all without a word from the group eating and arguing.

With a plate of steaming lasagna, Harrison sat at the table of women—Sera's women. As far as he could tell, she had done an amazing job with every single one of them. From the oldest all the way down to Violet, they were a reflection of the woman he loved.

CHAPTER TWENTY-EIGHT

LETTING the girl's conversation flow around them, Sera realized she had no idea what Harrison was thinking. She was so used to the constant hum of noise, but he wasn't. And she was sure he wasn't thrilled that the conversation always turned to things that the younger girls shouldn't hear about.

Maybe he would buy that they were not normally like this, but he had seen them at the party weeks ago, and they had acted the same way. Lucy and Buzz were discussing men they may or may not have gotten busy with separately, and Harper was telling Maby about the week's event schedule. Emma was sulking that Harrison was there, and Agatha was staring intently at Sera.

Sera gave her daughter a half-smile and a nod at the silent question floating between them. Harrison becoming a part of the girls' lives would change Agatha's the most; she had been a second mother to them since they were born. Even though Emma didn't need her as much anymore, they were still closer than the rest of the kids.

Agatha's dark eyes drifted to Violet and back to Sera again. Would her daughters lose the special bond that they had formed the moment Violet had been born now that Violet's father would be in the picture?

Agatha had been her only child to be in the delivery room with her that day, and she had also named the tiny baby. It was a name that hadn't even been on Sera's radar—she had decided months earlier on Ella. That day had bonded them together as more than just mother and daughter if that was even possible.

Each knew the others' secrets better than anyone else, but Sera had felt Agatha was drifting more and more these last few months. Not that she hadn't been able to find her footing since graduating from high school. For years, she had been nearly out of control, partying and getting into trouble. Then that had all stopped, and she did a one-eighty and didn't leave the house unless she was working. Sera hoped that adding Harrison to the mix didn't send the younger woman further into herself.

Pushing her plate away, Agatha leaned back and smiled at Sera, reassuring her that she was okay with this. Whatever this was.

"Cliff is at the Grog. Who's in?" Lucy said, looking at her phone longer than necessary to read such a short text.

"I am, even if it is Cliff." Harper got up, and so did Buzz.

Lucy followed as they put their dishes in the dishwasher.

"I'm out. I can't stand Cliff," Maby said from the table.

"You would love him if you just got to know him," her twin said.

"I'll still pass," she replied but got up anyway.

"Me too. I have to work at midnight. I just want to get some drawing in before I have to go." Agatha followed the rest in cleaning up after herself.

"I would go, but I know I'm not invited." Emma got up with a dramatic sigh.

"I'd invite you, Em, but mama bear pretends you are all innocent. I was getting served there when I was your age." Buzz gave her little sister a side hug.

"You were seventeen, and Lucy served you. Not a real waitress." Sera pointed out.

"I was a real waitress!" Lucy took offense.

"I'll watch a movie with you, Em," Maby said as the group headed into another room, some for the TV and some for the door or stairs.

The room was quiet when the front door slammed shut in the

distance. It was just the three of them, alone. Sera had no idea what to say to him. She knew that throwing him in the middle of all the girls was going to be a lot, but he knew what he was getting into when he stayed for the meal. She just wished the girls would have toned down their conversation, just this once. And it was made worse when Violet got up and wandered into the living room, leaving her alone with Harrison, who was just a chair away from her and not saying anything.

"Should I question whether any of what was said was true or not? Or just accept that they don't lie?" Harrison pushed his empty plate away from him.

"It's mostly true, I'm sure. No need to lie." She got up and took Violet's and her plate to the dishwasher.

"They weren't trying to impress me?" He followed suit because she wasn't cleaning up after him. She wasn't his mother.

"I don't really think anything they said would impress anyone."

Grabbing her around the waist, he pinned her to the cabinets. Pressing his body to hers, he said, "Everything they said impressed me. Two of your kids own their own business, one has a master's degree, one is a reporter for the biggest paper in town, and one is an artist that you had a silent conversation about me with. You are a fucking amazing woman. I can't wait to see how my kids turn out."

"I didn't do anything but let them be themselves. I am not my mother."

"Thank god, because she's a bitch." He kissed her forehead.

"She is. I was never good enough for her, or Father. I never wanted any of my kids to feel like that. I guided them; I didn't tell them."

"It worked. Now tell me about your unusual marriage."

"I married Bradford because I was pregnant with Emma. I knew my parents wouldn't like it, but they didn't like him either." She struggled against his arm. "After about three weeks, he went to South America to teach abroad. He was a literature professor."

He kissed her neck at her silence. "And?"

"And I haven't seen him since. Not once. He calls every year to check on the kids but really doesn't care. I stayed married until Buzz graduated high school so that I had a claim to her; to them all. I started to have sex again when Emma was a year old. I never really considered myself married. You were the only man I ever slept with at work, and it was just that once."

"I wish I remembered. I would have gotten rid of Veronica to be with you."

"You loved her, Harrison."

"I wanted what I thought she could give me, but I don't think it was ever love. I have never felt for her half of what I feel for you. When I'm away from you, you are all I think about. You are everything I want in life—you and our girls. And all those other girls that come with you." He couldn't let her go, even now.

"I have seven kids, Harrison. I will always have seven kids," she reminded him.

"I don't care. Although, I am hoping we don't have to live with them all forever." Nuzzling her neck, he breathed her in, knowing that she wouldn't be the woman he loved without all her kids.

"They sometimes move out," she said on a sigh, her hands running up his sides.

"I should start introducing them to my friends." At this point, he liked all the girls but didn't really want to live with them all.

"No pushing my kids. When they fall in love, it'll be on their own timetable." She pushed at his chest, but he didn't budge.

"Like their mom?" he whispered in her ear and felt her shiver.

"No, she's been in love with the same guy for years. He just never knew it." Her arms pulled him closer to her, not wanting him too far away.

"He knows it now." His mouth finally landed on hers.

Hours later, after they watched a movie with the kids and put them to bed, and after she had taken him to her bedroom, and they had made love, he had woken her slowly with kisses down her body.

She opened her eyes to see the man she loved, and he smiled at her. "See? I wake from a dead sleep just to look at you."

"You're just horny." She stretched, because she was too.

"That too, but I can't get enough of you. You will marry me."

"You have to ask, Harrison." Sera grinned, but he knew she loved when he was forceful.

"Seraphina Lovely Dean, will you marry me?" he asked, kissing her body between every word.

"I'm not a Dean yet." She giggled at his presumption.

"*Yet.*" Was the last word he said as his mouth claimed hers.

CHAPTER TWENTY-NINE

ONE NIGHT of sleeping over at Sera's house had been enough for Harrison. There were too many women in her house. There were females everywhere, and they weren't quiet. After the group came home from the bar at close to 3 a.m., he hadn't been able to fall back to sleep, though Sera wasn't bothered by it at all. She hadn't even stirred at the voices coming from the hallway just beyond her door. He hadn't lived in a house that wasn't silent at night since college. Every little noise woke him up, and there were a lot of little noises.

During the hours that he had spent lying awake with her sleeping in his arms, he had decided he couldn't live with her here, and she probably wouldn't want to move her kids into his condo. There wasn't enough room for two growing kids. He wanted his kids to have a house, just maybe not this one.

As the sun was just starting to lighten the dark night, Sera stealthily slid from his arms. Her movements were slow at first, and he didn't notice that they were coordinated and not just her moving in her sleep. Letting her go, he watched as she sat up and stretched her naked body before turning back to look at him.

"You're up," she whispered when she caught his eyes in the dim light.

"As are you, it's only five." He ran a hand down her spine. Her bed was small and cozy compared to his. Not much room.

"Saturday. It's time for breakfast." Was her explanation as she kissed him on the lips before going into the bathroom, leaving him alone in the bedroom.

If she was getting up this early on a Saturday to make breakfast for all these girls, she really needed to get a place away from them. Sitting up, he found his underwear and pants on the floor and pulled them on before she came out of the bathroom. She was dressed in loose lounge pants and a yellow T-shirt.

"You can keep sleeping."

"I'll help you," he offered, looking for his shirt.

"No help needed, Harrison. It's early."

"I've been up for hours since the bar crew came home."

"Sorry they woke you. Sometimes they can be loud. They try not to be. I'll talk to them."

"Sera, wait. I need my shirt, and I'll come with you."

At his words Sera, stopped and turned at the open door, then leaned against the frame as she watched him. What she was thinking, he had no idea, and she didn't say, just watched him as he looked around the room for his clothes.

There was more light in the hallway, and it illuminated her form. The hint of the curves he knew were there was enough to make him bring her back into the room and explore them again.

As he got up to do just that, his hand landed on his shirt. At the shift, he saw the expression on her face, and it said he would not be getting her back in bed right then. Pushing off the thought, he held up his shirt. "Found it. We can go now."

"Harrison." She stepped back into the room and closed the door, leaving them in darkness again.

"What?" he asked, her tone had him sitting back on the bed. Was he in trouble? Why?

She walked over to him and put her hands on his shoulders, "Breakfast is sort of a girls-only event. Always has been. It's a way for everyone to get together at least once a week and catch up."

"Sera, you all live together. How much catching up is there?" Not to mention the fact that she had seen all of them last night and spent time with them. How much more time did she need?

"Yes, we all live together, but we don't always see each other. Agatha works at night, and Maby and I work during the day. Harper works basically from the middle of the night to late evening with time off between. Lucy works midday to the middle of the night. Buzz works any hours she can. Weekend mornings are our time."

"You just saw them all last night," he reminded her and pulled her into his arms.

"Fluke. We don't usually get that." She tried for a second to push from his grasp, then stopped and let it happen.

"Can I stay?" he whispered into her ear.

"Uhm, no boys allowed, Harrison." She ran her hand up his check.

"How about I help you until someone wakes up?" he asked because he wanted to spend as much time with her as he could. It had been a long few days without her near him. They needed to make up that time.

"Help?" Her voice was incredulous, as if he couldn't help her in the kitchen.

"Help you make breakfast. I can make the bacon while you make the eggs." He kissed her neck. "I can make the sausage while you make the pancakes."

"Why are you making all the meat?" Sera giggled as she tilted her head so his lips could find more places to touch. "Besides, I don't make breakfast,"

Behind her, there was a pounding on the door. "Sera, breakfast is ready. Kick your man out and come down."

The sound made Harrison jump. He was sure that everyone in the house was sleeping but them. It might be why he had assumed that Sera would be cooking, that and she was the mom. Except there were two trained chefs in the house and five adults that could do it.

"Buzz," she whispered.

"There's no way they're already up." He stood up straight in surprise. Most of the women had only been home for around two hours.

"Yes, they are." She turned and opened the door again.

As she went down the stairs, he followed, listening to the voices coming from the kitchen. They weren't quiet and subdued at all, considering the time of the day.

"Told you he was still here," Harper stated loudly as he caught sight of nearly everyone in the kitchen.

"I didn't say I thought he was gone. I said I thought *she* would be gone," the redhead argued.

"Why would she still want to be here this morning? I for one would never be caught dead with a man in this house," Agatha said from a stool. Harrison noticed she was the only one wearing the same outfit she had on the night before.

"Don't you mean men, Ag?" Harper stated.

"Jealous," Agatha shot back.

"Morning, girls," Sera called to them,

"Morning, Mom," they all called in unison.

"Harrison, you want something before you go?" Harper asked, turning from her sister to him with a smile. A welcoming smile for a girls-only event.

"Sure," he answered before Sera could kick him out.

Walking into the kitchen, he knew immediately he had made a mistake, as all eyes turned to him. Three of the women shifted seats, leaving one open right in front of Harper and her spatula. The friendly offer wasn't friendly at all. This was an interrogation.

"Morning, ladies," he said, wishing now he had just stayed in bed like Sera had asked him to.

"Cinnamon roll or pork chop?" Lucy asked. He knew it was Lucy because she was helping with the food. He knew it was going to take time to actually tell the two apart. Last night, it had been easy to tell them apart when they were sitting and not moving around. Now they were dressed alike and seemed like they were trying to be identical twins.

"Pork chop," he said, knowing she was testing him but not what the correct answer would be.

Lucy smiled and filled a plate for him, then looked over at her twin and winked.

"Do you have any kids, Harrison?" Buzz asked from beside him, her red shirt with the word Buzz spelled out in orange letters clashing vibrantly with her red hair.

"No," he answered like always, then stopped and smiled. "Actually, I have two daughters. I recently met them."

"Oh, I hear a scandal. Does Sera know about this?" Buzz was nearly bouncing in her seat now.

"Yes, she does," Sera answered for him. "Where are Emma and Violet?"

"Sleeping," Agatha stated because she would have been the one to know.

"We will have to talk to them today," Sera added and touched his shoulder.

"I will have to talk to my mom also." Harrison took her hand in his.

"You have a mom?" Buzz asked. "Can I call her grandma?"

"Buzz," Sera's voice held more humor than warning. Oddly, it had been Buzz who had wanted to call Harrison dad also.

"Do you have siblings?" Buzz ignored her mom. "I need some hot cousins. Or hot uncles ... hot uncles would be awesome."

"I'm an only child," he told her, and the disappointment on her face was enough to make him smile. "What happened with Brad?"

If she could ask invasive questions, so could he. And he hadn't heard anything about him since the wedding fell apart. Maybe they were dating, and he just hadn't heard.

"Who?" Her face was blank at the name.

"The *groom?*" he reminded her, trying not to smile at her reaction. Poor Brad. It hadn't been that long since the engagement had been canceled. Though to Harrison, it had been a lifetime.

"I forgot about him. I think he was looking more for a serious relationship, hence the wedding. I just didn't feel it." She shrugged, turning back to her breakfast.

"Or did you feel it but are no longer interested?" Mabel asked with interest, the college professor.

"Ha ha. It's not always about sex, Maby." Buzz shoved a forkful of cinnamon roll in her mouth.

"When was it not about sex, Buzz?" Harper asked from the stove.

"Why is this suddenly about me? Sera brought a man to breakfast," Buzz argued through the food in her mouth and pointed to him.

"God, him again!" Emma groaned from the doorway.

"Emmaline." Sera turned to her daughter, jumped up, and gave her a hug, which the teen fought her way out of quickly.

"Aren't you over him yet, Mom?"

Walking back over to him and taking his hand, Sera announced to the entire room, "Nope, and I think this is going to last."

Half the woman in the room chuckled and repeated sarcastically, "*Last.*"

Agatha got up from the table and set her plate in the sink, turned to the room, and stated, "Welcome to the family, Harrison. It's not always easy to be a member of it, but it's well worth it." Then she left the room and headed up the stairs. Not a backward glance at the entire room left staring at her, open-mouthed in shock. Instantly all eyes went from Agatha's retreating form to Harrison to Sera and back to him.

"Holy shit!" Lucy stated more under her breath then anything.

"Girls ..." Sera started.

"You're getting married?" Emma demanded.

"I did not say that." Sera stated.

"How else do you become part of a family, Mom?"

"Emmaline Rose Lovely." Sera's voice took on the stern mom cadence Harrison now knew that came directly from her mother.

"Seraphina Marlo Lovely!" Emma mocked her.

"Now they're bringing out the big names," Harper announced, taking a step back.

"I don't like him, and I'm never going to like him," Emma yelled dramatically and even stomped her foot once.

"Emma, stop."

"I will not. You can fuck anyone you want, but you will not destroy our family. And that is all this is: you destroying our family." Emma turned and ran, her steps loud as she fled up the stairs until he heard a door slam.

"Emmaline," Sera sighed.

"I'll go talk to her." Harper threw down her spatula.

"No, Harps, I will." Maby got off the stool.

"*I will.* She's my kid," Sera said to them all and pulled her hand away from Harrison's as she left.

"She'll get used to it." Buzz punched him lightly in the arm. "Change has always been hard for her."

"Remember when she started high school and nearly ran away?" Lucy said, putting pork chops in plastic containers.

"Nearly? She was gone for like five hours. And then I spent the entire morning with her on her first day, so she didn't bolt again. High school math still sucks." Mabel poked at her pork chop.

"How about when we decided to get a real Christmas tree instead of that old plastic thing we always used?" Harper started gathering up empty plates from around the room.

"You mean the year of two trees?" Lucy laughed and shook her head.

"I think you and Mom are in for a battle with that one." Buzz punched him again.

Harrison took in their words and thought it would be a battle worth fighting. If she was anything like her older sisters, her dedication to those she loved would be fierce. Each would do anything for the other, and that included his own daughters. They all went above and beyond for Sera's girls, it seemed, and that was something Sera had taught them all.

"Why do you guys call her mom sometimes and Sera sometimes?" he asked the women. He had noticed that the names were oddly interchangeable.

"Because she is not our mom, but Emma was a wee bit confused when she was really little. For a month when she was three, she called her Sera, so we started calling her mom. But she is our mom," said Harper. The rest nodded in agreement.

When he had met Sera's girls last night, he had been impressed with them. They were accomplished women who seemed to know what they wanted in life. But today, he had seen a side of them that he loved, the part that had taken on a stepmother and stepsisters without hesitation and made them feel like a part of their family, a big part. He just hoped they would do the same with him.

CHAPTER THIRTY

DECIDING against knocking on her daughter a door, Sera walked in, happy she had taken the lock off the door when Emma hit puberty. It had worked well with the older five, so why not with Emma also? Not that she had had many reasons to come into her room. Emma was not a Lovely in that regard.

"Can we talk, Em?" Her daughter lay face-down on her bed, her head on her pillow.

"No," came the muffled response.

"What was that? I think I heard a 'yes.'" Sera walked into her daughter's room. Sera knew that the pale blue walls were not her daughter's favorite or even close, but Emma never said anything about it. None of her kids mentioned if they liked or didn't like their rooms after Sera had decorated a decade before. Emma had yet to put up a poster of any kind. That might have been because her daughter wasn't into posters or maybe she remembered the poster battle of a few years before, when Harper had pulled every single poster off the walls after someone had ripped her Gordon Ramsay one. Posters were not a topic to bring up, even today.

"Mom, you can just leave and spend more time with your boyfriend." Emma sat up and leaned against the wall behind her bed.

"Emma, you know I won't replace you." She sat down and squeezed her daughter's knee, seeing her anger for what it was.

"It doesn't matter, Mom." Her eyes said something completely different, though.

"Yes, it does, honey." She took her daughter's hand. Her first baby, who changed everything in Sera's life, now she thought that her own mother could just forget about her when a man came into her life.

"Are you going to move in with him?" Emma tried to shake her hand away, but Sera held tight.

"I don't know. We haven't talked about that," she admitted. Sera knew she wanted to be with Harrison and knew he wouldn't be comfortable here, but she didn't think she would be comfortable moving into his condo when there wasn't enough room for their girls.

"But you will."

"Yes. As will you because you are my daughter, and I will not leave you behind."

"What about your other daughters?" There it was, the change that Sera finding love would cause her daughters. Emma saw it right away. They all did, but Emma was the most affected by it.

"They are all adults, Emma. When you are an adult, you can also live away from me." She squeezed her hand. "Just not far."

"Mom." She rolled her eyes, her dad's eyes.

"Em, you know that I would do anything for you. Anything. But I am going to live my own life. That includes falling in love with a man and moving in with him. Living with him away from this house." She hoped Emma would understand. She hoped Emma would want her to be happy, even if she only had a teenager's insight.

"But why him? What is so special about him?" Emma tried to shake the hand off again and failed.

"I have no good answer for that one. All I know is it has always been him."

"But you just met."

"No, we have known each other for some time."

"I know. You work together."

"A little more than that, Em. We met in college."

"You never said that." Emma replied in surprise, as if that made all the difference to her.

"I was keeping that to myself." Sera squeezed her hand.

"Did you date then?"

"Not exactly."

"What does that mean?" Emma's eyebrow went up in question, a new Emmaism that Sera was starting to get used to.

"We sort of talked once or twice and then slept together," Sera admitted, trying not to blush but failed.

"You slept with someone you barely knew?" Emma's eyes were wide in shock, which almost caused Sera to laugh. Hadn't this kid paid any attention to the conversations around the house? It happened all the time, and everyone talked about it.

"I did." She hoped this wouldn't send her teenage daughter off on a spree of one-night stands just because her mom had done it. Sera wondered if she shouldn't have told her.

"Do you know how dangerous that is? You could have caught something or gotten pregnant!" Emma lectured her mom as if she was the mom.

"I do, and I will not do it again." She kissed her daughter's forehead and hugged her. "I did get pregnant. With you. Harrison is your dad. That's why you look so much like him."

It was the first time she had ever told her daughter anything about her father. Emma had never asked. Not once. Mostly it had been a relief to not have to answer questions that Sera didn't want to think about much less talk about, but she wondered if her daughter had ever wanted to know and just didn't ask. Nobody in the house had a dad, after all.

Emma shook her head at the admission. "I do not. What about Violet? Where's her dad? Now that you're suddenly telling everyone about dads, where's hers?"

"In the kitchen. You two share a dad."

"Why didn't you get together with him years ago? Where has he been for all these years?" Emma demanded. The anger was back.

"He was married, and I was married." Sera thought it better tell her everything, or she would have more questions later. Hopefully, fifteen was old enough to hear all the details.

"Mom!"

"I'm not proud of myself, but you're old enough to know the truth."

"I don't think I am." Emma looked at the ceiling and closed her eyes.

"Too bad, honey. You're a Lovely." Sera kissed her forehead again, then ran her fingers through her hair, relieved that one of her daughters knew the truth. "Now come down when you're ready. I have to tell Violet and maybe the big girls."

"They don't know?" Emma's eyes snapped to her. Sera told the big girls nearly everything.

"Nope, just you and Agatha."

"I am the second person you told, after Ag?"

"Emma, this is a big part of you. Agatha has known since Violet was born. Harrison found out yesterday. So, I guess it's up to you to tell the big girls. I want to tell Violet."

"Me?" she asked in wonder.

"You, Em. I think Harrison and I will take Violet out for breakfast, and you can tell the big girls. They'll enjoy hearing it from you." A plus from that plan was that Sera could put off the interrogation she knew was coming her way. The Lovely sisters didn't even know that the little girls shared a dad.

One last squeeze of her daughter's leg, and she left Emma alone. Emma was going to love being the one sharing what she knew about Sera and Harrison's relationship with her sisters. Especially since the sisters always knew more than her, at least until today.

In her room, Sera changed into jeans and headed down the stairs. In the kitchen, Harrison was still on the same stool, listening to her daughters go on and on with stories about everything and everyone.

"Harrison, I think you and I and Violet should go out for breakfast," she announced, stopping Lucy in the middle of a story about Sera that neither Violet nor Harrison should actually hear the end of.

Mostly Harrison because Violet wouldn't understand what Lucy meant.

"Didn't we just eat?" he asked, looking around the kitchen that was still filled with breakfast items and remnants of the meal that had been eaten. He looked comfortable with Violet was on his lap, who was currently still eating a cinnamon roll as fast as she could.

"We have something we need to talk to Violet about, and nothing is open but restaurants right now. So, breakfast it is." Sera pulled the plate away from her daughter, who nearly growled at her.

"Okay," Harrison shrugged and agreed. With his daughter on his hip, they headed for the door, Sera calling goodbyes and pushing him as they went. Not that any of the sisters said goodbye back; they were all just staring at their retreating forms.

Outside, he took her hand and stopped. "What was that all about? How can you still be hungry?"

"I'm letting Emma tell the girls …" Sera stopped because she didn't want to tell Violet yet. "And we're telling V."

"You told Emma without me?"

"Yes, she was angry and hurt, but I knew she would be. But now she's better about it. I felt letting her tell the big girls would make her more excited about it. You can tell Violet if it helps." Sera stated, her eyes not looking at the girl, as if that made her not there.

"Tell me what? What does Emma know that I don't?" the little girl demanded from his arms.

Both adults ignored her, and Harrison hissed, "It doesn't. I wanted to be there. I have missed fifteen years of her life, Sera. Now I missed another thing."

Taking his face in her hands, she kissed him. "I'm sorry, Harrison, but I have to take her feelings into account before I consider yours. For now, I understand their wants and needs more than you do. One day, you will too."

"What is Emma telling? I want to know too!" Violet demanded and forced him to put her on her feet, which were shoeless because of Sera's haste to leave.

"How about we go eat, and Harrison will tell you everything," Sera said to the girl.

"Why can't Emma tell me since she's telling everyone else?" the little girl demanded of her mom.

"What if we go out, and you can order anything you want?" Harrison asked Violet.

Sera glared at him. Was he offering rewards without consulting her first?

"I'm not hungry." Violet folded her arms.

"How about a toy store?" he suggested.

"Harrison!" Sera turned on him. "Do not bribe her. Is that all you have? Buy her stuff?"

"I've never dealt with kids before, remember?"

"You can't just bribe them. If you do, then every time you want them to do something, they will want something in return." Lesson one in parenting, it seemed.

"Kids understand that it doesn't work that way."

"Because you're an expert on kids?"

"I could have been, except I wasn't allowed."

Sera looked at her wrist, which didn't contain a watch, and snarled, "Less then twelve hours before you brought that up. I said I'm sorry, but I told you why I didn't tell you."

"I still missed a lot of time with them. They don't even know me." His words were barely out of his mouth before Violet rushed from the house and slammed into him in a hug. Sera hadn't even noticed she had left.

Harrison instantly dropped low and hugged her fully for the first time, and Sera's heart melted at the sight—a sight she had been sure she would never see. Suddenly, nothing he did was wrong. He was a great father.

"Are you really my daddy, Harrison?" Violet asked him. The smile on her face went from ear to ear.

"Yes, I am, Violet. Is that okay?" His voice cracked even though he could tell she was excited about it.

"Yes! I have always wanted a dad, and you are very nice, so I am glad it's you." She hugged him again.

Emma flew out of the house and looked at the scene in front of her. "I am so sorry, mom! I didn't even know she was there. I was explaining everything to the girls, and there she was. Did she hear everything?"

Sera gathered her into her arms and kissed her cheek. "It's okay. She's taking it pretty well."

Harrison looked up from Violet and said, "Let's go introduce them to my mom. She's going to love them."

"I guess since everyone has eaten already," Sera replied, grabbing Emma's arm, who looked ready to bolt.

"We're going to grandma's, everyone," Buzz called over her shoulder from the doorway.

"Not everyone, not today. Let's ease her into the Lovelys," Sera said. Nobody needed her seven girls showing up unannounced on their doorstep before eight in the morning. That was too much.

"But by Christmas, right? I bet she makes a ham." Buzz was nearly dancing.

"I make a ham!" Harper said indignantly from somewhere behind her. "What's wrong with my ham?"

"I just think a grandma would make it better. Your hams are just, meh. Grandmas always make the best hams. And cookies," Buzz said and was suddenly gone from the doorway as it swung shut.

"Let's go. No need to see what is happening in there," Sera replied and started for her car, praying Harrison would follow. The girls usually got loud when they were fighting, and Buzz's remarks had definitely sparked an altercation.

"Yeah, no need," Emma agreed with a grin. The teen knew exactly what was happening inside.

Sera smiled as she walked arm and arm with her daughter to the car, and Harrison carried their other daughter. Harrison pointed to his car, and Sera decided that since it was his day, so she would let him drive.

Slipping into the passenger seat, she wondered if they all would be here together now if Kylie Nash hadn't made her accusation. That suit was what had made him see her for the first time as something more than the HR director, as someone who had been there the entire time and would be there forever. She just felt lucky that she and her girls were beside him now.

CHAPTER THIRTY-ONE

HARRISON KNOCKED on his mother's door, knowing it was earlier than he had ever come over before by several hours. But he didn't want to wait to share his excitement about his kids. Now that everyone knew, he wanted his mom to know too.

While Sera had been with Emma, the Lovely sisters had regaled him with stories of his daughters and Sera and their family. They were a closer bunch than Sera had ever admitted. The older ones knew so much about even the littlest one that Harrison longed to know. They also knew way too much about Sera, so much more than he thought he ever would.

Now he stood on his mom's front step with Sera beside him, still in a bright yellow T-shirt that said "Yalling Stan" on it, which Sera had told him should say Yellow Stone, except Lucy couldn't spell and had produced dozens of shirts with misspelled words on it that everyone wore—mostly with pride and a little bit of fun.

It was early, and he knew he should have called, but calling would have wrecked the surprise, and he knew his mom wanted this to be a surprise. *Grandkids.*

"Harry, what are you doing here so early? And Sera, right?" his mom said when she answered the door, still in her bathrobe.

"Hey, Mom, can we come in?" he asked as she swung the door open farther.

"You may. It's early, though, Harrison. I haven't even gotten dressed yet." She waved her hand over her bathrobe.

"Go ahead and change, Mom. We can wait."

"Hello again, Sera," his mom said as if she had forgotten she had already greeted the woman.

"Hello, Emily. Sorry we dropped by so early. We should have waited until a decent time. Harrison wanted to talk to you right away," Sera said.

"Mommy did tell him to wait, but Harrison wouldn't listen," Violet said as she pushed her way between her parents and into Emily's house as if she had been there hundreds of times.

"And who are you?" Emily stopped her retreat into her bedroom to change to look at the little girl, still barefoot and in her pink princess pajamas.

"Violet. Who are you?" Violet asked, not even leery of the woman she had never seen before.

"I'm Harrison's mom, Emily."

"My sister's name is Emmaline. I like that better than Emily. I have an Emily in my class in school, and she is mean. Are you mean?" Violet said.

Emma had chosen to remain in the car, something that Harrison couldn't seem to bribe her out of, and Sera figured that one grandchild at a time was better than two. After Violet had charmed the woman, Sera would get Emma.

"I am not. Are you mean?"

Violet giggled and said, "No, I'm Violet."

"Do you want a cookie?" his mom asked, which was the perfect question, based on Violet's reaction.

Jumping up and down a little, she nearly yelled, "Yes!"

"How about a hug?" His mom was already walking back toward her.

"I guess if I get a cookie too." Violet let his mom hug her tight. Over her little shoulder, his mom mouthed, *Yours?*

Harrison just nodded. Of course, his mom would notice the resemblance right away. His mom quickly led the little girl into the kitchen. Changing her clothes had been completely forgotten.

"How did she figure it out so fast?" Sera asked, amazed.

"Violet looks a lot like I did when I was young, and so does Emma."

"Don't I know it. Those two are like your clones, but girls."

"And you didn't even hint that they were mine," he said to Sera. It still stung a little that she had hidden them from him, especially after he met them.

"I had my reasons." Which he could tell she wasn't getting into again.

"Mommy, do you want a cookie?" Violet came back towards them, carrying two in her hand, one half-eaten.

"I do, Violet," Sera told her daughter before taking the cookie from her.

"Did you bring your other children?" Emily asked Sera, finally taking her eyes off her granddaughter.

"Just Emma. The rest are still eating at the house." Which he knew wasn't true because they were done before they had even left the house. He was happy Sera hadn't pushed to bring all the girls to meet his mom. The two younger ones needed to meet their grandma alone.

"Where's Emma?" Emily looked around the house, but Emma was still sulking in the car.

"Violet, why don't you and I get Emma, and then we can look at Emily's pictures of Harrison when he was little. There are some really cute ones," Sera asked her daughter.

"Okay, Mommy. I'll get Emma, and you can start snooping." Violet slid off the stool and ran out the front door to get her sister. Sera wandered into the living room, giving them time together.

This left Harrison alone with his mom—his very upset mom. Her arms were suddenly crossed, and the smile was gone. For some reason, he knew he was in trouble for something he didn't do.

"Harrison, I might not be all that great with math, but that girl was born when you were still married."

"I can explain."

"No, 'she's not mine,' then? No excuse that what I am seeing isn't true?" Emily sat down on a kitchen chair and patted the one next to her.

He carefully sat next to her. "She is mine. I just found out yesterday. I had no idea."

"Sera never told you? And you're okay with that?" Emily demanded. It seemed like she wasn't okay with it at all.

"I was married, and she was married. I didn't remember it even really happening, but it was during a bad time in my marriage. I can believe it happened ... I wasn't a great person during that time. We've talked about it."

"Oh, you talked. Well, then, missing years of your kids' lives is okay."

His mom was right. He *should* be mad, but he had made mistakes also. Would he have believed Sera if she had told him she was pregnant after the Christmas party? Would the revelation have prompted anything but anger and hurt feelings? He had been back with Veronica by the time Sera would have found out. And Veronica would in no way have wanted Violet in their lives. Finding out then would have driven a wedge between them years ago that would still be there today.

"Mom, I'm not missing any more of their lives. We both made mistakes. I should have let Veronica go a long time before I did. Instead, I tried to hang on to something that was already over, and in doing so, I left Sera to shoulder the burden of our children alone. I should have noticed Sera for who she was. *Is*."

"And who is that?"

"My life, Mom. I can't see my life without her now. I am going to marry her, and we will raise our kids together."

"You only have one, Harry. Maybe get used to one before you start planning more," Emily stated wearily.

"Two, mom. Emma is mine too. She's fifteen. Sera and I also met in college. It was just a one-time thing." He knew he was blushing. Even after all these years, talking about sex with his mom was awkward.

"And she knew that girl was yours the entire time? And went on to have another child with you. And still not didn't tell you about it? Are you even believing this, Harrison?" Emily leaned back in her chair and shook her head at him.

"Of course I am, Mom. I've met Emma, and I've met Violet. And I believe it because I know Sera; she doesn't lie."

"She just doesn't tell you about your children."

"Because I was married and trying to stay that way. Sera let me do what I thought I wanted," Harrison explained.

"I wouldn't have divorced my husband when I was pregnant with Violet anyway, Emily," Sera said from the doorway. "Buzz wasn't eighteen yet, and I would never risk her going into the foster system. I had raised those kids for years, and I wasn't letting them go; I'm still not." She held Violet in her arms with her head resting on Sera's shoulder, and Emma peeked out from behind her.

"Why didn't you just tell him? Didn't he deserve to know?" Emily turned to the woman surrounded by her grandkids.

"Yes, but at the time, I couldn't guarantee he wouldn't just take my children from me and walk away. Everyone in the office knew he and Veronica were having trouble conceiving. What a gift if I had his child. And could I even fight it? I was a single mother with six children and no husband in sight. Add to that the fact that I had no money to spare. I couldn't have hired a lawyer even though I worked in the same office as them. My divorce went through a small-time lawyer who barely got it done, and it was not contested. I would have lost my child."

"That wouldn't have happened." Harrison was on his feet. All this time, he had seen her life as it was now, not seeing her from back when she had been pregnant and alone. How many of the older girls had been in college at the time? How many mouths was she still feeding every night and day?

Sera set Violet on her feet, ignored him, and kept talking to his mom. "I couldn't take that chance, Emily. Not with my children."

"What about when you were here, and you knew he would not take your children?"

"I wasn't a hundred percent sure he liked me for me, or if it was because I was in charge of his investigation." Her words came out in a hushed whisper.

"What?" He took a step back from her. How could she have not known what he was feeling for her was genuine?

"What Investigation? Are you a killer or something? I knew there was something off about him." Emma said sarcastically from behind her mother.

"Stop, Emmaline," Sera whispered, ignoring most of what her daughter said. "Sorry, Harrison." Her eyes locked with his in a silent plea for forgiveness.

"How could you believe that?" He was trying to control his anger but knew he was failing.

She finally turned to him. "How? Because until the investigation started, you had no interest in me at all. We had known each other for ten years and suddenly, you didn't hate me? Hard not to separate the two."

"Then why did you …" He stopped and looked at his mom and then his daughters, who were watching him in interest. Too much interest.

"Because I have loved you for most of my life and for a moment, I wanted you to love me too. I was selfish. Which is why I never told you about the girls. I was selfish and wanted to have a part of you in my life … even when you hated me," Sera said as tear ran down her cheek. Then she turned, and Emma stepped away so Sera could flee.

"Sera," he called and was surprised when she actually stopped. "From now on, I will be selfish. I want to spend as much time with the girls as I can. I want them to know I'm their dad and that I love them."

"I understand." Her head fell at her words.

"And I want you there for the same reason. I love you and want to spend as much time with you as I can." He rushed toward her, past Emma, and took her in his arms, Violet and all.

"I won't leave my children," she muttered into his shirt.

"Yes, you will. The older girls are adults and want you to be happy more than anything. I'm not stopping you from being their mom and loving them, just living with them. We need a place of our own. Just remember, you would want them to move out one day, too, right? When they find the right one?" Her head nodded into his shirt. "You need to go first. Show them how it is done. That's what moms do."

"Your condo is too small," Sera whispered.

"Then we'll find something bigger. Someplace we both love. That we all love." He included his daughters, because all his decisions would be about them from now on.

"Why do we have to move?" Emma whined from behind them, making Sera laugh.

"Because you have to live with mom and dad, Emma. Everybody knows that!" Violet yelled at her sister.

"No way. I already have a room and a home. I will visit when I want to," Emma argued, her arms folded in anger.

"Not a chance. I have missed fifteen years of your life, and now I get to live with you for fifteen years. It's only fair." He pulled away from Sera and looked at their daughter, who was still standing slightly behind her mom.

"I'll be thirty then! I'm moving out when I am eighteen like normal people. No way can I put up with Sera until I'm thirty!" Emma protested.

Without even planning it, he let go of Sera and pulled Emma into a hug, his first with his oldest daughter. She was going to be tall and was thin and perfect. Except for the curse she emitted, and that her entire body was trying to get away from him instantly.

"Normal? Isn't your sister thirty and lives at home? And the rest seem like they are staying. From what I've seen, Lovelys live at home forever." He held fast to her because he knew the instant he let go, she would retreat back behind her mom.

"Not this one." She actually kicked him in the shin, and he let her go. Nonchalantly, she straightened her clothes and glared at him.

"Good thing you're a Dean. Then you can forge your own path," Sera said, grabbing the teen into a hug herself. This time Emma went willingly.

"Am I a Dean?" Violet asked with excitement.

"Yes, you are, sweetie," Sera said.

"I am not. Not ever. You can ruin our family, but there is no way I'm changing my name," Emma hissed and pushed out of her mom's arms.

Despite knowing Sera would be mad, he tried another tactic. "Emma, if you change your name, I'll buy you a car for your sixteenth birthday."

Sera glared at him.

"Deal, Dad!" Emma's face broke into a smile as she took the bait instantly, but her words still warmed his heart. "You know it's next spring, right? And I already have my permit."

"Can everyone excuse Harrison and I while we have a small talk?" Sera pushed Violet towards Emily and turned to Harrison. Silently, but with a bounce in her step, Emma went willingly with her sister. It seemed he had found the perfect prize to dangle in front of her.

Sera's nose was flaring already, and her chest was heaving, and he knew he was in for a fight. Taking her hand, he led her through the door before she yanked it from his grasp.

Once the door slammed, she stomped her foot. "Did you seriously promise her a *car*? I told you not to bribe the kids, Harrison. What are you going to get her next? A college education? A house? All for what? You've opened a can of worms with that one."

Smiling, he let her rant, letting her get it out of her system as he enjoyed the show, like always. He still loved to watch Sera Lovely get mad.

"And what are you going to get Violet? Surely she will need something just as big and bold."

"Are you done?"

"No, I am not!" she stated but didn't say anything else.

"I will buy her a car, and I will pay for her college education and a roof over her head because I am her dad and because I've been missing from her life for a long time. So, next summer, when we share a last name, a home, and a life, I will gladly take her out and buy her an old Jeep because that's what she'll want."

"You don't know that." But Sera's words weren't in anger. That was gone and had been replaced by a soft look as tears formed in her eyes.

"I think I know her well enough that she will want the same as all her sisters. And we will both say yes, and you will show her how to fix it and take care of it. In our garage at our house." With his thumb, he caught the tear that fell from her eye.

"How did you figure her out so fast?"

"Her sisters told me a lot about her this morning, but mostly because she's like her mom. I love you, Sera, and I love our kids."

"Me too. You and our kids, I mean." Her arms wrapped around him and pulled him tight to her as her head rested on his shoulder.

"Could you maybe let me make my own mistakes in this parenting thing? My mistakes might look like I haven't thought it through, but sometimes they'll be made in hopes of my kids learning to like me or to spend time with me. To love me, too." He held her and ran his hands down her hair.

"They will love you, Harrison. Just give them time." She reached up and kissed his lips.

Behind them, the door opened. "Grandma says to stop making out on the front step. She has neighbors, you know." Violet's stuck her head out the door in accusation.

Sera looked around the front of the house and saw nobody was out and looked back at her daughter. "We'll be right in."

Violet closed the door. Through the door, they could still hear her say, "They won't stop. I told you. They are probably going to have BBCBS."

Laughing at her daughter and knowing she would never be able to look at Harrison's mom in the face again, she whispered, "So a while back, you called me a sexless prude. I would like an apology for that one."

"I am sorry, Lovely. I hope that you never become a sexless prude and that our daughter never learns what BDSM is."

"With this family, she'll know before she's ten." Sera sighed. Her kids were terrible at oversharing.

"But you wouldn't trade them for anything." He leaned in and rubbed his nose with hers.

"Now that I have you, not a chance." Sera gave him a kiss, one for the neighbors to talk about, because being the talk of the neighborhood was nothing new to her.

EPILOGUE

SHE HAD BEEN STALLING. That was her only excuse to why she had barely moved anything out of the Lovely house. Slowly over the last few weeks, she had moved most of her clothes and almost all of her personal possessions to the new house, a house that she had loved on sight, and Harrison agreed to because it was the first one she had even liked a little.

But today was her wedding day, and her stalling had worked until right now. No longer did she have the excuse that she needed to periodically run home for something, which was how she had moved so much over the course of only a few months. After today it should all be gone, except it was already gone.

So far, Harrison hadn't said anything about it. They were already basically living together, except the one or two nights a week she spent at the Lovely house. She was ninety-nine percent sure that they were in this forever, but that one percent didn't want to come back to no bedroom.

"Are you sure you want to do this?" Agatha asked from the doorway. Today she was wearing a gray sweatshirt with matching sweatpants. Sera held her tongue because she knew by the time the wedding started, she would be in a dress. She had better be, at least.

"Yes," Sera said without hesitation. Her time for stalling was over.

She grabbed the bag she had packed off the bed. In it held everything she needed to get married that day. Tomorrow would be soon enough to admit to Harrison that she had almost nothing in the house, that she had been staling, just like everyone had been saying for months.

It was before dawn, but she was already showered and dressed in blue jeans and her favorite blue Kantaty shirt. Today was the day. Not for the big move; that would come later, but today, she was becoming Mrs. Harrison Dean. Yes, she was taking his name—no way was she not since it belonged to Harrison. After spending sixteen years as a Lovely, she hated to leave the name behind, but her two kids were now Deans, so she would become one too.

Harrison's bribe had worked, and Emma had agreed to the change before she got the car, which was just as well because she was looking at far more pricier ones than Harrison had dreamed of. But that girl had her dad wrapped around her finger and would be getting whatever she wanted—the same with her little sister.

"Are you sure? We could be in Kansas by the time anyone misses you." Agatha grinned casually, leaning against the door frame.

"How fast can you drive?"

"Faster than you, Mom." Agatha grabbed the bag from her.

"You look tired. Are you sure you want to go with me this morning?" Agatha dodged her fingers as she tried to push her bangs from her eyes, which meant she wasn't interested in a hug, even if it was Sera's wedding day.

"Yes. This is our last chance to be just us before you get married." Agatha frowned at her and headed out the door.

"We will still be us after I'm married." Sera followed closely behind her.

Agatha started down the stairs. "Not the same."

Agatha's words were true. From here on out, Sera wouldn't be there every day to see her girls, to guide them and be a big part of their lives. From now on, she would just be an observer in their lives. Still the mom, but different. The overwhelming sadness that the change brought was why she came home, no matter how much she loved Harrison.

"I know. Maybe I shouldn't be getting married. Harrison would understand." Sera stopped on the top step and knew he wouldn't. It was quite possible that he was looking forward to this wedding even more then she was.

"Harrison might, but not any of the two hundred guests you invited." Agatha finally realized she wasn't following and turned to glare at her.

"Once I started, I had a hard time stopping," Sera admitted. Maybe she had gone overboard, but she was only getting married once. Well, twice, but the first one didn't count. Except for her kids, she had gained nothing from that one.

"I noticed," Agatha teased her and started down the stairs again, not waiting any longer.

"Wait until you get married, Ag. The entire town will be invited." She followed, teasing her daughter.

"Not getting married, so not actually happening. Thank god."

"I'm going to love watching you fall in love."

"I'm not. So, why do you have to be at the church so early?"

"I don't. I just need to do a few last-minute things." Sera was never going to admit to her daughter that she wanted to be there early so that the day would get over earlier. As much planning and preparing she had done, she wanted it over already. She was tired of it.

"So, you have no reason to actually be there at five in the morning?" Agatha handed her bag back to her with a frown.

Sera glared at her and stated, "I want to, Agatha. Isn't that reason enough?"

"I guess since it is your big day." Agatha pointed at the white Jeep parked on the street. "Let's take yours. But I'm driving because I drive faster."

"That is exactly what I'm looking for this morning, Agatha. Speed!" Sera yelled as she walked backwards toward her Jeep, though she had thought it was in the driveway last night. Someone must have taken it during the night, a night when they were supposed to be sleeping. Well, if they weren't listening to her yet, they never would. They had better not be tired at the wedding.

Planning her lecture, she opened the door and slid into the passenger seat, then looked at Agatha, who hadn't left the front porch yet. In fact, she had sat down on the top step and was waving at her.

"What the ...?" She started to get out of the truck when a hand on her arm stopped her.

"Shut the door, Seraphina. We're going for a drive," Harrison said, causing Sera to actually follow his request.

"What are you doing here, Harrison? We were not supposed to see each other before the wedding! It's bad luck." And more importantly, it wasn't on the agenda.

"Relax. I just have something I want to do before we get married and start our lives together." The streetlights were turning off as he pulled up in front of Rodgers and Associates, in the parking lot she always parked in. Now he either parked next to her, or they drove together.

"Work? You are taking me to work?" He took her hand as they walked into the quiet building.

In the three months since Harrison's investigation, things had improved for her. Three of the partners had retired in the wake of the new rules that Sera had created, Keith being the first of them. Two had also been forced to resign because they hadn't thought that the new rules applied to them. At least they had done so before a complaint could actually be filed, but just barely.

As far as she knew, Kylie was still in town, but she hadn't heard anything about her. Nobody had, as far as she or Harrison knew, though it would have been nice to talk to her about Josh Rolf or even talk to the man himself. Not that Harrison wanted a relationship with his half-brother or anyone from that side of his family. Just some understanding of why he was set up would be nice.

Looking back on all she knew about Kylie, Sera worried about her a little. Maybe it was because of how close she had come to being like her, to being desperate and unable to rise above the bottom.

"Yes, because I have something that we need to do before today."

As the elevator took them to their floor, his body hovered so close to her that she could barely breath. After all these months together, he could still make her breath stop just by being near her. If they weren't in the building that they both worked in, she would demand he kiss her. Touch her. Do it all at once.

Once the doors were open, he backed away from her and slowly led her toward the conference room. The building was empty and eerily silent as they walked. Him walking backwards, and her fallowing. Him silent and her unable to be silent any longer.

"Why are we here, Harrison? Have you rethought a prenup? I thought you didn't want one? I was all ready to sign last month, but now I think I am a 'no' on that. I'm not going to let you divorce me, so why be afraid of it?"

"I told you, my money is your money, and your kids are my kids. Even trade."

"So, you bought my kids?" she said with a grin, just like the last time he said it.

"Yes, every one of them." He held up eight fingers because he was always teasing her about how he couldn't keep them straight or remember how many there were.

"I haven't thought about how much per child you paid. I think you underpaid. They are worth a ton, so you might need to take out a loan." She giggled at his frown. "A big one."

"Quit arguing with me. Why is it that when we are in this building, you are always arguing with me?"

"Because you think you're better than me when we're here. I need to remind you that you are not." It wasn't exactly true. She just loved arguing with him, and at work, he couldn't win by taking a shortcut and getting her naked.

"That's not how I feel." He tugged her into the conference room down the hallway from their offices.

"Good. At least you are changing."

"Maybe a little."

"Where do I sign?" She looked around the conference room. Now that the lights were on, she saw that the table was completely clear and there were no papers on it.

"There isn't a prenup for you to sign." He pulled out the closest chair and rolled it away from the table.

"Why are we here then?" She frowned at the room; it looked the exact same as it always did. Though since the meeting about his conduct had taken place in here, they hadn't both been in here at the same time. She wondered if she should be nervous until she looked into his face.

"Because, Seraphina Lovely"—he lifted her onto the table—"you once accused me of having sex in this very conference room. Since that day, I have thought of nothing but having sex with you in here."

"You want to have sex in *here*?" She looked around skeptically. Sure, she had thought about it before. But acting on it?

"Yes, with you, before either of us are married again." He slipped his hands under her shirt and unhooked her bra.

"Uhm, I'm not exactly comfortable with this." She said the words but let him slip her shirt and bra off her body anyway. The thrill sent shivers up her spine, and it wasn't just because Harrison was there.

"Yes, you are." His hands were busy with her pants as he kissed her neck.

Letting him do the work, she smiled and grabbed at his shirt, pulling him to her. "I am. I *so* am."

Her laughter filled the silent room until it turned to moans from both of them. It broke so many of her rules, but worth it—it had been a fantasy of hers, too.

She finally had someone who understood her completely. Someone who knew her inside and out. Someone who was her one true love. Harrison Dean.

EPILOGUE

THREE MONTHS Later

"IS BEA WITH YOU?" Chelsea King asked in disappointment as Sera Lovely walked into the house. The younger woman, who opened the door after only one knock, wasn't interested in seeing the potential buyers at all.

"No, she's busy," Sera informed her, even as Chelsea looked out the door beyond Harrison, who hadn't even made it past the threshold yet, just in case Sera's stepdaughter was there.

Not that Sera knew if her stepdaughter was busy or not. Bea hadn't shown any interest in looking at the house, which Sera didn't understand. All of her kids should want to see the house she was interested in. After all, this might be the place that would finally be good enough for her to move away from them.

Sera looked around the house again. It was dark and not nearly as inviting as the Lovely house, which was just two blocks away, but Sera could see beyond that. She could see fresh paint on the walls and bright, comfortable furniture. It would be a home for her family, but not the entire family. Harrison had said only their daughters would move in with them; the others had to stay at the Lovely house.

"Is anyone else coming?" Chelsea asked, and her shoulders slumped when she shut the door behind Harrison.

Turning to her fiancé, she saw that he wasn't impressed. She didn't care if he couldn't see the potential; she could. After just a short time together, she knew he liked things already nice and shiny. He didn't want to bother with things like renovating.

"So, why are you selling?" Harrison asked the young woman.

"My parents passed on last year. Both of cancer, just weeks apart. I just can't stay here anymore." Chelsea ended in a whisper as she leaned against the door.

Sera could see her eyes sweep the room and wondered if she was seeing her parents there. Pushing away the need to wrap her in a hug, Sera focused on the house and not the girl.

"Sorry about that, Miss King," Harrison said and reached out and patted the woman on her head.

Sera tried not to laugh at him and his discomfort when confronted by an emotional woman. She couldn't decide if he was uncomfortable himself or just didn't know how to comfort someone. There was still so much she needed to find out about her fiancé.

"Can we just look around, Chelsea, or did you want to do a tour?" Sera asked, hating that she was giving the girl an option. She wanted to wander and tell Harrison how they could and would make the home theirs. With an emotional homeowner with them, that would be impossible.

"I can show you around, but it probably isn't that much different from your house. Not that I've been in there," Chelsea said, straightening up.

"Oh, I thought you and Bea were friends?" Sera asked in interest since she had asked about her stepdaughter. Buzz never talked about the girl, but they were close to the same age and had to have known each other for years.

Chelsea looked out the glass of the door and said, "Yeah, we are friends. Just not 'visiting each other's houses' friends. Nothing like that."

Sera only nodded. They weren't friends at all. If she had been friends with any of the girls, Sera would have seen her at least once, even if it had been years before.

"I see. Can we just look around the house?" Sera tried again.

"No, no, I'll show you around. So, this is the living room. As you can tell, there are hardwoods in here, but they might have to be refinished. I'm not sure what condition they're in." The woman pointed at the floors.

As one, Sera and Harrison looked down. There wasn't an inch of hardwood flooring visible; the room was wall-to-wall rugs. Most didn't even match, and they were layered on top of each other, making the floor very uneven. Sera only hoped that the rugs had protected the floors because they were a trip hazard.

"The rugs are a nice touch," Harrison said, his tone indicating that he had no idea what to make of the things.

"Thanks, I can leave them for you. I don't know where I'm moving to yet. If I need them, I'll have to take them." Chelsea led them from the room into an equally carpeted kitchen. It has been redone at some point around the time Chelsea had been born. Or it had been started because half of the upper cabinets sat on the lower cabinets. But the style hadn't been popular in two decades.

"Looks like you're renovating," Harrison said as he looked around, not touching anything. Sera could tell she was losing him on the house.

"My dad started, but Mom got tired of all the dust, so he quit. You get used to it quickly. Plus, everything is easily reached." Chelsea opened a cabinet, touched the top shelf with ease, and smiled.

"And more rugs," Harrison pointed out.

"Mom hated cold floors, and Dad didn't like carpet. It was a compromise." Chelsea smiled and headed out of the room.

Sera could tell who wore the pants in Chelsea's parents' marriage. She just hoped that she had as much control over Harrison as that woman had over the man who had lived in this house. It was the only way she'd get the house.

"How many bedrooms?" Harrison asked as they carefully went up the stairs. Though there was no carpet or rugs, it was lined on both sides with baskets full of an assortment of items: yarn, blankets, other baskets, even one full of puzzle pieces. Just clutter, making it only possible to walk up them single file.

"Four, not counting the master. No, five. I forget that the junk room is a bedroom."

"There's a junk room?" Harrison asked, his eyes still focused on the baskets on the steps.

"Of course, where else do you put all the stuff that doesn't fit in the attic?" their leader asked as if Harrison's question had been obvious.

"How many siblings do you have, Chelsea?" Sera jumped in, not wanting to hear Harrison question about the clutter any more.

"It's just me. I was their miracle baby. They had been trying for twenty years before Mom got pregnant with me." Chelsea smiled as they made it to the top of the stairs.

"Wow, that is amazing. Did they ever tell you their secret?" Sera asked, glancing at Harrison.

It didn't seem like he was even listening as he stared at the floor-to-ceiling paintings of some sort of roman scene based on the attire of the people, or lack of attire, because everyone was very obviously naked. There were a lot of people lounging around eating grapes. It was all Sera could focus on—grapes.

"Who painted this?" Sera asked in disbelief. From one end of the hallway to the other were naked Romans. Then back up the other wall was a mirror image of the first.

"Tildor Qvist Ek, have you heard of him? Very famous. This was his last masterpiece. Mom loved it and would spend hours staring at it." Chelsea smiled at the wall before her.

"I can see why." Harrison then turned to Sera and shook his head, his eyes telling her he would never, ever step foot in the house again.

Chelsea shrugged and replied, "I can't say I love it. I'm used to it, though. It's been in here my entire life, but sometimes it's creepy."

"That's the word I was thinking," Harrison said under his breath.

Sera looked over at Chelsea, glad she hadn't heard. She was concentrating on the erotic painting and not on the couple who would be painting over it. Sera hoped it wouldn't take too many coats of paint.

"So ... bedrooms." Sera tried to get the tour back on track. She was losing Harrison more and more with every minute spent in the house.

Chelsea shook herself back and said, "Yes, we have the master here." She pointed at the closed door but didn't stop. Instead, she rushed to the door on the other side of it. Sera understood her inability to go into her parents' room; they hadn't been gone long, and the family had been close.

When she opened the door and stepped in, she announced, "This is Audrey's bedroom."

Sera chuckled at the name until she looked inside. There were dozens of posters of Audrey Hepburn, from signed pictures to movie posters. There was no bed but three life-sized mannequins in clothes resembling the movie posters.

Taking a deep breath, she walked in. "The room is a nice size, isn't it, Harrison?" He wasn't paying any attention to her. "I think Violet would like this one. A little paint is all it would need."

Which was true. Once the Audrey collection was gone, it wouldn't take much to make the room ready for an eight-year-old. There was a window seat, and Sera could see Violet sitting there, just watching the world outside. Or pouting about something, which was what was actually going to happen. Violet wasn't one for people-watching.

"I don't know. Audrey has been here so long.... I think I should leave everything so that she's always here."

"I think you need it where you end up, Chelsea, as a reminder of your parents," Sera hurried to say before Harrison could say anything. He definitely wasn't loving the Audrey room. It was just another strike against her house.

"Maybe there's another room," Harrison stated in his best lawyer voice, the one that showed no emotion—the one Sera had always hated.

"Sure thing." Chelsea took one more look around and headed out of the room.

Harrison grabbed Sera's arm and stopped her from leaving. His dark eyes looked into hers as he stated, "No."

"Give it a chance, Harrison. It might grow on you." Shaking off his arm, she marched from the room, knowing he would follow because he wasn't getting trapped in the Audrey room.

"This is Dad's hobby room. Mom wouldn't let him carve anywhere else. She hated the mess it would create," Chelsea said and opened the door to the cleanest room they had seen yet. There were no rugs, no carpets, no clutter. It seemed the dad wasn't the problem.

Stepping into the room, she admired the perfect hardwood floors and the wainscoting that was lost everywhere else in the house. The room was gorgeous ... until the wall of shelves containing the carvings came into view. Each was of a very intricate and perfectly proportioned cat. All the cats were in a different pose, if only slightly. Some were big, some were small, and there were thousands of them. Maybe more than that.

"Cats?" Harrison gasped, his eyes on them.

"Daddy loved cats, loved them. But Mom was allergic, so he never could have one, so he carved them. Each one has a name on it." Chelsea was nearly crying.

"They're good," Sera said. It was the truth, just overwhelming.

Wiping a tear, Chelsea started heading out of the room. "I can leave them if you like them. I don't know what I would do with so many. Dad never wanted to part with any of them, and I don't think he ever did. Every one he made is all right there."

"Cats," Harrison said again, his eyes still on them.

"Emma would love this room, with the dark woodwork and the view of the back yard." Sera tried to cover his shock.

"Maybe you want to look at my room before you decide. It's the best room in the house, which was why I had it." She hurried out of the room.

Harrison was reaching up to touch a cat when Sera knocked his hand away and gave him a stern look. No cat touching. Then they hurried after the woman with the crazy parents.

Before she could catch up to Chelsea, who was going into a room down the hallway, Harrison rushed out and immediately opened the next door. Sera stopped and stared into the room. It was completely full of boxes, all the exact same size and stacked almost to the ceiling. There was a walkway to the window, and that was all the floor space visible.

"You found the storage room," Chelsea said as she sped back to them. "That is all my stuff; my toys from when I was a kid, and every piece of clothing I have ever owned. Mom hated to get rid of it, so I still have it."

"*All of it?*" Sera couldn't help but ask.

"Yes, I can leave it for your girls. That way, you'd never have to buy them anything again. Unless they grow taller than me," Chelsea stated, which made both her and Harrison look over at her. The woman was almost six feet tall, which was unusually tall for a woman, and there was no way either of their kids would grow that big. Emma was still on the short side at fifteen, and Violet had always been small for her age.

"I enjoy buying clothes for the girls," Harrison said.

Sera glanced at him with a smile. So far, he hadn't bought them anything. Either he was planning on it, or he was finding a way to not end up with every item of clothing Chelsea King had ever worn. Sera hoped it was both.

"Too bad. You can't see much in there, but it's kind of small."

"An office then," Sera announced before Harrison could call it "the reason they didn't buy the house."

Harrison harrumphed and turned to the next room. It seemed he was tired of Chelsea's tour and just wanted to be done. Opening the door, it was a nice bedroom in oak with a gray comforter. It looked like any bedroom in a normal house but was completely out of place there.

"Your room?" Harrison asked, even though there wasn't a lick of femininity to the room. It was a man's room through and through.

"No, it is Tildor's room. Mom didn't want it disturbed in case we needed to turn the house into a museum," Chelsea stated.

"Tildor?" Harrison asked in confusion.

"The artist?" Sera asked. That was the only one she had ever heard of, and it had been from this woman.

"I knew you had heard of him! You might want to keep the room like this, just in case," Chelsea said with excitement.

"Uhm, we'll have to talk about it," Sera replied, knowing exactly how that talk was going to go. "So, when was the painting created, in case I'm ever asked?"

"The year before I was born. It took months to complete. Tildor stayed right here in this room the entire time. Mom and Dad loved having him here. She talked about it a lot. But he died before I could ever meet him," Chelsea said, her eyes staring back to the hallway.

Looking around the sparse room, Sera would mention nothing about how strange it was to keep a shrine for a man for over twenty years. Or that there might be a simple explanation of her parents' "miracle" baby.

Instead of anything else, she said, "That's too bad."

"It is. I wish I had just met him once. With his paintings all over the house, in some ways, I feel I know him."

"More than the hallway?" Harrison asked, and Sera noticed him give a visible shake at the thought of more.

"Yes, there's a painting in the master. It's gorgeous, and I want to keep it. But if you two love it, I could leave it," Chelsea said.

"No, we couldn't possibly keep it if you love it," Sera stated, hoping that it wasn't a full-on mural again, but if Chelsea could take it, she was sure it wouldn't be.

"So, your bedroom?" Harrison asked. They were at the end of the hallway by the room Chelsea had slipped into earlier.

"I thought that your teenage daughter might like this one. I have always loved it," Chelsea said and led them into a pink room, so very pink it hurt the eyes. There was pink carpeting, walls, and floors. Even the ceiling was pink. The bed had a canopy, and it was in pink ruffles —so many ruffles.

Sera was sure that her daughters had never had this many ruffles total in their lives. It was overwhelming.

"Pink," Harrison said and backed out of the room.

"I'm sure that the girls will fight over the room," Sera said to the woman, hoping to get into her good graces. In reality, her girls would fight to stay *away* from the room.

"I understand."

"Sera," Harrison said from the hallway where he was back to looking at the painting. A very nice-sized penis was eye level right outside the door.

"The house is very nice, Chelsea. Harrison and I will have to talk about it. It's a major purchase, after all, and our first together. We don't exactly have the same taste," Sera told the girl, but she was sure that there was no way to get Harrison to buy the house. There was just too much work that would have to be done and too much of everything that he wouldn't be able to look past.

"I understand, and I know that you don't want to move out with all your kids at the house. Kids are supposed to move away, not the parents." Chelsea led them back down the stairway to the front door.

Harrison took Sera's hand and leaned towards her. "I would rather live with your stepdaughters than here."

Which was saying a lot because he hated staying with her daughters and hadn't since the first night. No matter what she promised to get him to stay, he always went home. There were too many women in one house for his taste.

Sera had thought that it was the perfect house when they had walked in. It was the perfect location and the perfect size, and she had learned to love old houses after living at the Lovely house all these years. But she had to admit this one was just too much, even for her.

We haven't seen the master," Harrison said from beside her.

Sighing, Sera realized that she didn't even want to look. There was no telling what oddity was hidden behind that door. These people were just a step beyond kooky.

"Oh, yeah," Chelsea said and went to the door, opening it. "There is a large walk-in closet and a bathroom. That was added just before my parents bought the place."

Resigned to knowing what the couple's bedroom was like, she first noticed the picture. It was of the same roman scene, but the couple looked more like Chelsea than those in the hallway. But they were equally naked. The positive was that it was just a picture hanging above a fireplace and not a mural.

"Does the fireplace work?" Harrison asked, finally sounding excited about something in the house.

"Yes, I think so. Mom liked a good fire on a cold day," Chelsea replied.

"I do too." Harrison started looking over the fireplace.

Below them, a sound went through the house. It sounded like a door opening. Chelsea turned in excitement. "That might be one of your daughters. I will go look."

Before Sera could tell her it wasn't one of her daughters, the woman was gone. She hoped that Chelsea wasn't getting her hopes up that any of her stepdaughters were going to be her friend because Sera would put a stop to that if it happened.

"I don't think it works. I mean, it could be fixed if it doesn't, but I don't think it does," Harrison said.

"How much do you know about fireplaces?" Sera asked. He had an electric one in his condo, nothing like the one he was in front of.

"Not a lot, but enough to know that this one doesn't work." Harrison got up and crossed his arms as he leaned against the non-working fireplace.

Sera took the time to look at the bathroom that seemed small but okay, and the closet that was huge. The room was bigger than hers down the street, though far smaller than the one in Harrison's condo.

"We are not moving here, Sera. Not a chance in Hell. The house is creepy and needs more work than either of us are willing to do to it," Harrison stated.

"Come on, paint and cosmetic stuff. That's all." Sera tried to fight back the tears that were threatening but failed. This had been the perfect house until they stepped inside. How could it have gone so wrong so quickly?

"It needs an exorcism, and that painting is creepy as Hell." He pointed to the picture above the fireplace, which might've been why his back was to the thing.

"Maybe you're right, and it needs more than what we want to do," Sera admitted as a tear slid down her cheek. Turning before he could see it, she looked out the window and could almost see the Lovely house. There wouldn't be another house this close.

"Of course, I'm right," Harrison said and walked over to her, pulling her into his arms, squeezing her to him.

Chelsea came back into the room in a rush, "Nobody was here. I thought may have been Bea. We're friends, you know."

"Yes, I heard," Sera said with disappointment and pushed away from Harrison's arms. "I think we have seen enough, Chelsea. Thank you for showing us around. When are you putting it on the market?"

"Next week, unless you take it," Chelsea answered with excitement.

"We will have to talk about it." Sera couldn't hide the sadness in her voice. Harrison hated the place and with good reason. It was awful.

"We'll take it," Harrison said at the same time as he wrapped his arms around her again, pulling her back to him.

"Really?" Chelsea asked in excitement.

"Really?" Sera asked in disbelief.

"Yup. It's perfect." He kissed Sera's head. "Did you have papers for us to sign, or should I get some drawn up? We want to close as soon as possible."

"I have some downstairs," Chelsea said, rushing from the room.

"What the hell, Harrison?" she asked in shock.

Harrison smiled at her. "This is the house you want."

"Which you just said you hate," she reminded him.

"You want to be right here, and I want to be with you. No matter what's wrong with this house, it's only two blocks from the house you really want. Your girls will be close. Not living here, but still close enough for us to visit. Just a short walk down the street. Everything else can be changed." He wiped the tears from her cheeks.

"But it will be a lot of work." She didn't go on with all of its faults; he was saying yes. No need to have him change his mind.

"And we will hire someone to do it. By the time we come home from our honeymoon, it will be unrecognizable. Just in time for us to be a family," he said and kissed her.

"This is going to be our family home." She looked around, seeing everything that would be changed before they moved in. Changed and made theirs.

"The Dean Family house. It has a nice ring to it." He pulled her into a hug and held on to her.

Wrapping her arms around him, she knew that if she didn't think he loved her before, she was sure of it now. Nothing but love would make him buy this house. How she had gotten so lucky, she would never know. But she would never take it for granted.

ABOUT ALIE GARNETT

I love to read and prefer a little spice in those books. I am lucky enough to live on a small hobby farm in northern Minnesota with her husband and two kids. I enjoy spending time in the pasture with my two mini horses and one fainting goat (who doesn't actually faint). When I'm not writing, I'm busy trying to do all the things I didn't get to while writing. Or maybe I wouldn't have gotten to them anyway, because its laundry, dishes and fun things like that.

ALSO BY ALIE GARNETT

Landstad, ND

Invisible

Irresistible

Impulsive

Insuppressible

Intriguing

Imperfect

Irreplaceable

The Great Lovely Falls

Falling for the Single Mom

Falling for his Best Friends Sister

Falling for the Boss

Falling for his Step-Sister

Falling for his Fake Wife

Falling into a Second Chance

Hart Series

Seeing her Pain

Her Favor

Max Valentine is Looking at Me!

Keeping her Safe

Stand Alone

Romancing the Doctor

Made in the USA
Middletown, DE
10 March 2024

51202537R00126